TRIAL RUN

A WILD HERITANCE TALE

S. LYNN HELTON

ISBN (Paperback): 978-1-7326763-6-7
ISBN (eBook): 978-1-7326763-7-4

Scripturio Books
www.ScripturioBooks.com
24.04.08

DEDICATION

To my family.

ACKNOWLEDGMENTS

Thank you to my first and beta readers for all the great suggestions.

CHAPTER 1

Namid snatched her hand back just in time to avoid getting caught. With a reminder to herself to act casual, she eased further into the market's bustle, frowning at the cacophony and the not-always-pleasant mix of odors. More than any supposed quality of goods, noise and smells characterized the open-air markets of Rhadanthus, especially in this ring of the decrepit city.

She wondered what had happened to her promised distraction. It would have to be a good one to attract attention with all the clamor. Had the other apprentices failed at their part?

Namid wove through the crowd while she nibbled at a piece of fresh bread, purchased with half of the few korz—the small copper coins of the Six Realms—that she carried. Without trying, she spotted several full pouches that she could snatch with no trouble. But her instructions today were to take from the merchants, a harder task. And so, the use of a distraction... *if* her fellow apprentices would ever get to it.

As she strolled, Namid scrutinized each market stall she passed, both sides of the street. She found little of interest, not unusual for the time of year. The merchants offered mostly goods they had made during the heavy winter storms, goods that held no attraction for her, especially that morning. She noticed rivals Biera and Surbhi both had stalls to sell their pricey nalbound hats, socks and the like. Namid glanced at the wares both women displayed but continued on. She hoped to find some tasty treats to snatch, something to relieve the monotony of the usual winter meals of pottage.

She shivered in the chill breeze that swept down the street and pulled her cloak tighter, brushing away strands of her shoulder-length black hair that caught in her eyelashes. When she spotted a City Warder stalking through the crowd, she drifted to the other side of the street and pretended interest in one merchant's meager selection of overpriced jams. Namid could not smell the sweet preserves over the odor of the fish from the next stall, fish no doubt caught from the small river that flowed through the city. She noticed several thin dogs lurking near the fish stall, probably hoping to snatch something, much as she hoped to.

Namid glanced at the fish and shook her head the slightest bit. While she had not tasted any fish in some time, she did not want to try to grab any to take back. No need to make a challenging task even more difficult by choosing something so odorous.

And she had no desire to smell of fish the rest of the day either.

From the corner of her eye she saw one of the dogs try to grab a fish, only to be chased off a short distance by the merchant. The dog simply joined its fellows again in a slow slink back toward the fish.

After the Warder moved on, Namid resumed meandering through the crowd and wondered where the others were. Maybe they got sidetracked. Or too into their own guises as legitimate buyers. Whatever it was, they had better remember their purpose soon. Namid was running out of goods that she could pretend interested her.

A disturbance from one end of the street drew her attention. She hoped it meant the other two apprentices had *finally* decided to do their part.

While the people in the street surged that direction to see the cause of the disturbance, Namid scooted back to the stall with the jams and grabbed two small jars. The merchant there had stepped a pace away from his stall and was straining to see the cause of the fuss at the end of the street. He took no notice of her at all.

Namid tucked the jars into the small bag at the back of her belt under her cloak and rejoined the crowd. She slipped in and around the throng until she reached the steps to one of the taverns. She climbed them to see better and focused on the scuffle near the end of the curved street.

She easily spotted two City Warders, nearly surrounded by agitated onlookers. The Warders struggled with two wriggling youngsters, a girl with brown hair in long twists and dark brown skin, and a boy with lighter brown hair and much lighter skin. Both wore faded tunics and trousers, simple in design, much like Namid's.

Zwena and Orran.

At the youngsters' feet lay several items from the market. The owners of the stalls that sold those goods shouted at the Warders about theft.

By the gods, really?! Namid sighed and shook her head.

Getting caught by Warders had to be the worst possible distraction the two could have conceived. Although, judging by the scattered goods, Namid doubted that getting themselves caught had been their plan. She hoped not, anyway.

Namid shook her head again. Unbelievable!

Today *she* was the one supposed to take things. Zwena and Orran were only supposed to have created some fuss to draw people's attention, after which all three of them would have disappeared into the small alleys that cut through this ring of the city.

Namid looked around. How to fix this fiasco?

While she tried to come up with something that had a chance of working, she spotted a small basket of spiced pastries sitting unwatched nearby. She took a quick breath-of-time to snatch it, then slipped into the nearest alley. A quick climb up the rough walls brought her to the worn rooftops and she found a cranny in which to hide the basket and the jams. Then she dropped back into the alley and returned to the street.

The struggle with the City Warders had mostly subsided and Namid's fellow apprentices stood held in place by the firm grips of the two Warders. The youngsters glared sullenly at the crowd around them.

More than a year behind Namid in their apprenticeships, Orran and Zwena usually worked well as a team. And usually followed directions. Namid frowned in their direction and wondered why—today of all days—they had decided to ignore what they had been told to do.

While they held Zwena and Orran, the Warders also spoke with the irate merchants.

Namid sidled closer as the others in the street returned to their original pursuits. She could not leave Orran and Zwena with the Warders. But how to free them?

She recognized both City Warders, but had not dealt with either of them, so an attempt to talk a way out of this for Zwena and Orran had little chance of success. And trying would bring her to the Warders' attention, an outcome she wanted to avoid.

If she could draw one of the Warders away…. Maybe that would give Orran and Zwena the chance to free themselves. She looked over the nearby merchants' stalls and smiled at an idea.

Namid set off back along the market street at a brisk walk, just slow enough to avoid unwanted attention. She tried to look nonchalant at the same time as she hurried.

As she passed Surbhi's stall she snatched one of the

merchant's prized nalbound hats and tucked it under her cloak. Then, while she passed Biera's stall, she tucked the hat into the goods that woman displayed for sale. With her setup complete, she returned to Surbhi's stall and edged in close to two women who stood looking through the merchant's creations.

"Why look at that! Isn't that the pattern I just saw on one of Biera's hats? Biera's nalbinding is *so* much better," Namid said in a loud voice, then melted back into the crowd.

With a screech of fury, Surbhi charged Biera's stall and found her hat there. Clutching the hat in one fist, she clambered over the table to attack Biera, all the while yelling at her, accusing her of stealing the hat, the designs and her customers. Biera screamed back at Surbhi that *she* was the thief and punched her in the face.

With a satisfied smile, Namid slipped through the throng that surged toward the fight. Again she climbed the steps of the tavern so she could see.

One of the Warders was heading toward the fracas, leaving Zwena and Orran with her larger companion. That Warder was a big man and he held both youngsters with the necks of their tunics bunched in his large hands. While they fought to get free, he still managed to maintain his grip, looking little bothered by the effort.

Namid frowned and looked around again, desperately trying to come up with something to get him to let go. Her gaze settled on the stall with the fish, where yet again the dogs eased close to grab something while the merchant tried to shoo them away and at the same time strained to see what the fuss further down the street was.

A glance around to make sure no one paid her any attention and Namid scurried over to the stall, staying behind the merchant. Wrinkling her nose, she grabbed several fish and waved them at the dogs.

Come on, she silently urged them. Here's some nice fish you don't really have to work for….

Finally she got their attention and they started toward her. She backed away, making sure they followed, then ducked into an alley that she knew would take her to where Orran and Zwena were held. She ran then, holding the fish out away from her clothes. Most of the dogs followed. She hoped she could stay ahead of them long enough.

She pulled up the hood of her cloak one-handed as she burst out of the alley. Ducking her head to hide her face the best she could, she charged ahead, right into the Warder's back, then slipped to the side while tucking the fish into the man's belt. As she wiped her fishy hand across the back of his tunic, the fish fell from his belt, trailing stinky slime down his trousers and boots in the process.

A breath-of-time of surprise was all he had before the pack of dogs engulfed him, noses eagerly searching his clothes and bodies tangling around his feet as they fought over the fish.

"Run," Namid urged her fellows as she dashed past, headed for yet another alley. "Else I'm of a mind to just leave you here."

She paused to look back before she ducked around the corner into the alley. Zwena and Orran managed to twist out of the cursing Warder's grip as he fought to keep to his feet while he tried to fend off the hungry, fish-loving dogs. The two youngsters each hurried away from the ruckus in a different direction. Namid ducked around the corner of her alley then headed for the rooftops.

She retrieved her jams and pastries from the cranny that hid them and made her way to the meetup that the three apprentices had agreed upon earlier. She arrived first.

She wrapped her cloak around herself to try to keep warm while she waited for the others. They joined her several breaths-of-time later.

"And just exactly what was that?" Namid greeted them.

"We just thought we could grab a few things, too,"

Orran said, with a whine to his voice.

"You clearly thought wrong," Namid said. "When we're given jobs like this, follow your instructions. Plenty of time later when you're full Shadowers to grab what you like."

"*If* we get to be Shadowers," Zwena said. "We have to prove ourselves, too. But how can we do that if we're only doing distractions?"

Namid shook her head. "Everyone works distractions as first-year apprentices. And having some skill at distractions can be very handy. Give it time."

She headed back home, Orran and Zwena trailing behind her, still complaining about doing distractions.

Namid hoped that the younger apprentices' actions had not ruined her chances, hoped she had done well enough on this last apprentice job that Dar, leader of the Shadowers, would agree that she was ready for the next step. She *felt* more than ready to prove she deserved a permanent place among the Shadowers, as this group of thieves and sellswords called themselves.

She smiled to herself. At least she was bringing back some treats that the Shadowers ought to appreciate.

CHAPTER 2

After she ate her midday meal in the cramped kitchen, Namid took herself to the large room on the main floor of the Shadowers' home, the place where they all tended to gather when not busy elsewhere with various tasks. She hugged tightly to herself the knowledge that Dar had just agreed she was ready for the next step. Soon everyone would know, but right then she wanted to savor it just to herself.

She found a spot at one table with Jaikrein, one of the full Shadowers she considered a friend. She plopped down her cup and took the dice the older woman held out to her.

Namid tucked some loose strands of her hair behind one ear and threw the dice. They bounced across the rough table and came to rest near Jaikrein's cup.

"Ten!"

Namid had to shout so Jaikrein could hear her over the noise of a score or more people gathered in the room. Most perched on benches at any of a bunch of scarred tables, dicing, just as she and Jaikrein were.

Jaikrein snorted but smiled at her. "Beginner's luck,"

she said as she laced one hand through her long, pale hair and reached for the dice with the other.

"Indeed," came a cool voice from behind Namid. "She seems to be filled with it."

Namid frowned. She had hoped that Aahmes would not find her there, had hoped he had somewhere else to be, something else to amuse him.

The dark-haired young man had acted unfriendly toward her, at best, since the day they had first encountered one another, the day Dar had taken her in after he caught her trying to steal some food from him that he had just stolen himself. Later, when Dar had accepted her as an apprentice, Aahmes had become just shy of hostile toward her, for no reason that she knew.

To make matters worse, many of the other Shadowers had teased the pair from the start about how much they resembled each other – with their straight dark hair, similar features, and red-brown skin. Bad enough that Aahmes seemed determined to undermine or hinder her at every opportunity, but he *would* have to look like he could be her older brother, too. Only a few years older, Namid guessed, not that it made a difference.

As Aahmes settled himself at the table, he met Namid's gaze, for once not sneering at her. Suspicion wormed its way through Namid at this unusual behavior. Probably he was too occupied planning something that would make her look bad to come up with one of his usual taunts. But if he was, she could not see it in his expression. He just watched Jaikrein's throw, a five and a three, without even the expected stinging comment.

Now Namid just *knew* he was planning something.

"You take that one," Jaikrein said. She pushed a few korz toward Namid.

Jaikrein then glared at Aahmes, who returned the look with an aloof one of his own. But she offered the young man the dice, if he wanted to play. Aahmes shook his head and gave Namid a speculative look.

And here it comes… Namid thought.

"Word is that you're ready for your Trial," Aahmes said.

Namid tried to hide her surprise. Not what she had been expecting. And how did he know that already anyway?

"So soon?" Jaikrein gave Namid a big, gap-toothed grin.

After Namid passed the Trial, a two-part test of her weapons-work and her thievery skills, she would be a full member of the Shadowers.

Namid grinned back and pointedly ignored Aahmes, hoping to irritate him into revealing what trouble he had prepared for her this time. "I've apprenticed for two years already, Jai."

"Aye, that you have. Who'll do the designin' for you?"

Namid shrugged. "Dar hadn't given me a list of Shadowers to choose from yet, when we spoke earlier."

"I offer my services." Aahmes gave her a wicked grin, the challenge clear in his expression.

Jaikrein looked startled and gave Namid an uncertain look. All the Shadowers knew how Aahmes acted toward her.

Namid pretended not to notice Jaikrein's look. Instead, she studied Aahmes, her eyes narrowed.

This was not at all what she had expected. Although perhaps she should have. What better way for Aahmes to cause her further trouble than for him to design her Trial? So what could he be planning?

Jaikrein shook her head. "Don't do it, Namid. If you have this one designin' your Trial, who knows what type of killin' test he'll come up with."

Aahmes gave the older Shadower a withering look. "I wouldn't come up with a Trial that was unavoidably fatal. But the Trial *is* supposed to test tyros' abilities, to see if they can hold their own and belong with us."

"That's a good one! You sayin' not 'unavoidably fatal',"

Jaikrein said. "But we all know you've had it in for her since the beginnin'."

Aahmes shrugged. "If she can't handle it, it'll be clear to everyone that she doesn't belong here with the Shadowers."

Namid gave Aahmes an overly sweet smile. "So *generous* of you to offer to help a lowly tyro such as me. I think having you design my Trial is an absolutely *wonderful* idea. Then when I pass, there'll be no question that I'm good enough. It'll be clear to *everyone*, as you said."

Aahmes looked surprised, like he had not expected her to accept. He studied her, his gray-brown eyes narrowed, then gave her a thin smile.

"I'm glad you're so enthusiastic about it. I'll let Dar know." He stood. "How soon do you think you'll be ready to begin?"

"Whenever you are."

Aahmes gave her a dangerous look and a toothy grin. "Say in a couple days' time, then?"

"Fine. I'll be prepared."

"I doubt that," he scoffed. He sauntered away, exchanging casual greetings with a few friends in passing.

Jaikrein watched Aahmes with a distaste she did not try to disguise, then turned to Namid with a frown. "Are you crazy? Have you not been payin' attention the past couple of years? You have to know he's out for your blood. Any test he's designin' will kill you."

"I don't think it's that serious." Namid tried to reassure the older woman. "He even said so himself."

Jaikrein snorted her opinion of that.

"He's just never liked me. We all know that," Namid continued with a shrug. "Probably 'cause I'm the first person he's met who's anywhere near as good as him with a blade. Not to mention thievery. But he hasn't tried to kill me, even when we've sparred. I don't think there's as much risk as you fear. And I'm willing to face the risk, anyway."

Jaikrein shook her head and gathered her dice. "It's a foolish risk. It won't prove anythin'."

She headed away from the table.

"I'm not trying to prove anything," Namid called after her.

Jaikrein just waved a hand at her but did not turn around.

She *wasn't* trying to prove anything, was she? Namid wondered. She pondered a few breaths-of-time, head tilted slightly as she worked through how she felt about the whole thing.

She had to admit that the notion of succeeding at a Trial designed by Aahmes appealed to her. How he would squirm when she returned triumphant! *That* would make the whole unpleasant business of having to deal with him worthwhile.

She amused herself with that satisfying image and nursed her drink until she received the expected summons from Dar.

CHAPTER 3

Namid dashed up the stairs to the tiny room that Dar liked to call his office, on the second floor of the dilapidated building the Shadowers called their own. Compared to the other structures in this rundown ring of the shabby city of Rhadanthus, theirs was a castle. In jest, they named it Shadow Keep.

Namid found the stocky leader of the Shadowers pacing in front of the table that served him as a desk. His auburn hair looked more disheveled than usual. He stopped his pacing when she entered and gave her a stern look, fists planted on his hips.

"Are you crazy?" Dar said.

She laughed. "That's just what Jaikrein said."

"And?"

"Maybe, maybe not." Namid looked away from his flinty gaze. "I intend to take Aahmes up on his offer, anyway."

Dar studied her face in silence for several long breaths-of-time. Then he nodded.

"I'm not going to be able to talk you out of this, am I?"

Namid gave him a look he knew all too well. "No."

"You planning on having him do both parts of your Trial?"

Namid tilted her head and considered. "I hadn't thought of having someone different for the different parts."

"It's something you can choose to do, if you want." From his expression, Namid felt he hoped she would do just that.

After thinking about the idea, though, she shook her head. "I don't think so. Aahmes for both the weapons and the thievery. It'll be better that way."

Dar sighed and shook his head. "You children and your absurd rivalry."

"I'm not a child!" Namid said. "And I didn't start...." She trailed off as she heard her own words.

Dar shook his head again, but with a grin.

"All right, I see your point," she said. "Still, I think this will best prove that I belong with the Shadowers." She gave Dar a sidelong look. "And just think of the fun everyone'll have wagering on a bout between him and me."

Dar shook his head yet again and gave her a resigned look. "All right, all right." He rubbed his forehead with one hand. "I now understand when my mother would say 'you'll be the death of me'. Because you two...."

Namid raised her hands in a warding gesture and backed up a step. "Yeah, us children."

Dar looked exasperated then. "All right. I'll accept Aahmes as your Trial designer. For both parts. Just keep in mind all you've learned, all that I've taught you. You'll no doubt need it. All of it."

"No doubt," Namid agreed in a dry tone.

"And, it being Aahmes, don't trust anything you might get from him, whether information or advice. Be extra vigilant."

She nodded.

"I spoke with Aahmes right before I called for you. He

says he's ready to tell you your thievery task this night—"

"When we talked earlier, he said a couple of days," Namid interrupted.

"I'll tell him to wait then." He gave her an expectant look.

Namid shook her head. "Don't. I've no objection to starting right away. In some ways, it'll be better than waiting and wondering."

"I suppose." Dar did not sound convinced. "After the evening meal, then, we'll make the announcement and find out what farce of a Trial he's come up with for you. I expect his first ideas to be unreasonable. We can also set the time for the weapons-work portion. But now you should try to get some rest. I wager you'll have little enough time for it after you learn what your Trial requires."

Namid nodded and turned to go, but his hand on her arm stopped her. She looked back over her shoulder, surprised at his unaccustomed expression of unease.

"Be careful." He pulled her into a quick embrace, then freed her and turned away from this atypical show of concern. "This'll be a hard Trial. Do me proud."

"I will," she said to his back.

Then she fled, like him, from the unusual display of sentiment.

~ ~ ~

After she left Dar, Namid found she had too much time with too little to do before the evening meal. She tried to rest, as Dar had suggested, but instead she lay wide awake on her bed—one of four in the small room she shared with Zwena—and stared at the ceiling. Her thoughts darted about like hungry birds chasing winged bugs.

She tried not to think about her feelings about Dar. His obvious concern touched her but unsettled her at the same time. While the Shadowers treated each other as comrades, sometimes as a large bunch of rowdy cousins, in general they shied away from forming any closer attachments to each other.

The leader of the Shadowers had been her mentor almost since she first arrived in Rhadanthus. He had steered her around the pitfalls of life in this place and guided her in learning skills she would need to survive. She shook her head at her musings. She did *not* need another father, or even a father surrogate.

Her thoughts turned to the Trial and all her misgivings jumped out at her. Was she rushing into this, as Dar seemed to fear? Was she letting Aahmes' animosity dictate her actions? She truly did not believe he had any desire to see her dead.

Injured? Yes, she saw him trying for that. Discredited? Even easier to believe.

But outright killed? No, not at all.

She got up and poked around her room with some thought of starting to assemble things she might need. Weapons... a good idea to have along in case plans went awry. Which they often did.

She paused at her small pile of clothes. She might need to have a guise or two ready to help her get into places in the city that her current faded and somewhat ragged attire would lock her out of. She dug through the small selection of garments she had, while her thoughts returned to concerns about Aahmes.

Why had she so quickly accepted Aahmes' offer? She could not deny that it would be a sweet victory to defeat a Trial *he* designed, maybe take down that superior attitude of his some. But these thoughts led her into an area she tried to avoid thinking about... her reasons for wanting to join the Shadowers in the first place.

True, being a thief was far better than prostituting herself, the other profession too readily open to destitute newcomers to this dangerous city. But stealing?

Even after two years of apprenticing as a thief, she still struggled with doubts about that. Sure, as part of her apprenticeship, she had picked some pockets and pilfered some small, not-too-valuable items from the wealthy nobles who lived near the opulent center of Rhadanthus. And greedy merchants, like earlier that day.

But the Trial involved much more than that. Could she slip into someone's house, the place they considered safe, and take something conspicuous and valuable, a treasure the owners prized? She paused in her digging and stared at the opposite wall to consider that.

The questions that always followed, when her thoughts turned this way, were easy ones.

Did she want to be able to eat? Without having to sell herself?

She smiled a grim smile and shook her head at her thoughts. She knew the answers, of course.

And beyond those considerations, the Shadowers offered her a place where she could be safe and anonymous. No one here cared about her past, about who she had been before she came to this city. An attitude just fine with her. Better than fine, even.

Something she needed.

And once she had proven herself, proven that she could pull her own weight, then she would be just one of the group, worthy of assistance and protection if the need arose, but otherwise just another Shadower. No one to attract attention, no one anyone need look twice at. She sighed and hoped it would be true.

She smiled when the call to the evening meal finally came, relieved to have her reverie interrupted. She did not feel rested but was able to put aside her qualms. At least for the time being. Without a second glance at her scattered belongings, she ran to see what kind of Trial Aahmes had in mind for her.

CHAPTER 4

The evening meal was noisy, as usual, with plenty of cheap wine and hot, if uninspired, food. At her table, Namid's companions toasted her anticipated success in her upcoming Trial while making wagers on everything possible related to it, including even what it might be.

As often happened in the Keep, the Shadowers already knew that she was ready for her Trial, ready to take on that last challenge to prove herself as one of them, although Dar had made no official announcement yet. Hard to keep anything secret in a building of skilled skulkers.

Namid smiled a lot and ate well but avoided the wine. She did, of course, lay a wager on her success. She also placed a wager with a different Shadower that Aahmes would first propose something completely impossible for her Trial. She expected to collect on that one with no problem. Beyond that, while she waited for the meal to end, she just watched all the Shadowers as they talked and laughed and wagered, enjoying the diverse community she hoped to soon belong to as a full member.

After most of the assembled Shadowers had finished their meals, Dar stood and pounded on his table with the pommel of his knife. Silence spread through the hall as the Shadowers gave their attention to their leader.

"Shadowers, in spite of some unsanctioned additional challenges, our Namid has successfully finished the second year of her apprenticeship," Dar said. He gave Zwena and Orran a frown that had them squirming in their seats, then smiled at Namid. "The gods willing, in the next few days, she'll prove herself and become a full Shadower. Not that she'll be done yet with her learning of Shadower ways." Here Dar gave Namid a stern look which she answered with a grin.

He paused a breath-of-time then continued, "If she accepts her Trial design, tonight marks the start of her Trial. May it end in success!"

With one hand, he urged Namid to stand as the Shadowers shouted their approval. Namid smiled at this show of support, and her face grew warm at the same time. When Dar raised a hand for silence, the Shadowers quieted.

"As you all know, the Trial will be of two parts, weapons-work and thievery," Dar said. "Aahmes has volunteered to serve as overseer of her Trial and design both aspects. Namid has accepted his offer."

Perplexed murmurs caused by this announcement ran through the assemblage while Aahmes stood and bowed to the room in general. He looked at Namid, who stood three tables away. A sudden chill swept through her at the predatory smile he wore.

Aahmes spoke loud enough for everyone to hear over the ongoing muttering. "To complete your Trial, beyond your weapons-work—which will be against me—your task is to steal and deliver to us the Star of Corentris."

Namid gaped at him as the room exploded into confusion. She was not surprised that he wanted to spar with her for the weapons-work. That, she had expected. But how could he have chosen the Star for her thievery?

The Star of Corentris was a statue, a sort of distorted

star-shape, which held a jewel said to be worth hundreds of navns – the gold coins of the Six Realms. The jewel might even be worth thousands. Stories said the statue came from some long-lost city far to the south. The statue was formed from some rare, prized metal, silvery in color but not silver.

The one thing that made stealing the statue truly difficult was that its owner, Chendrukhar, was a man with the Power that many called magic. He kept the statue in his walled stronghold to the east, just outside the city. All the tales claimed that its guardians were not human. And there were other considerations around stealing from the mage, such as how to keep the theft secret long enough to get any value from the stolen item.

From the back of the hall, Jaikrein's voice carried over the others. "I dispute!" she shouted.

Dar pounded the table again until the Shadowers quieted. "The Shadowers will hear this dispute," he said, "as is our tradition."

Jaikrein stood. "The thievery part of the Trial is supposed to be somethin' the overseer of the Trial can do. I say Aahmes can't do this theft. I doubt any of us could, alone."

A rumble of agreement passed around the room and left muttered discussions in its wake. Namid felt many eyes on her but she kept her gaze on Dar, who stayed silent for the moment. Then the Shadowers' leader gave a curt nod, perhaps seeing some confirmation of his own thoughts in her expression.

"Jaikrein has a valid dispute. Modify the thievery portion, or come up with another test," he told Aahmes.

"Wait!" Namid shouted.

Ignoring the quizzical look Dar gave her, she turned to Aahmes. "If I agree to this Trial you've devised, how long do I have to get the Star?"

"One night beyond this one."

Namid imagined she felt disapproval in the room, but

this time everyone only whispered to each other as they watched.

"I still say even Aahmes could not do this," Jaikrein said. "It willna be a fair Trial for Namid."

"I've already proven myself," Aahmes said. "Are you casting question on my abilities?" He dropped a hand to the hilt of one of his daggers and glared around the room.

Silence again spread throughout the hall. Although many among the Shadowers managed to only tolerate him, Aahmes was, without question, one of the most accomplished of them, both in thievery and with daggers.

Namid watched him with interest. If someone accepted his challenge, she welcomed the additional chance to study his knife-fighting methods. Especially since she would face him for the weapons-work portion of her Trial. So, she should learn all that she could. They were both good—and they both knew it—and she had already heard the rumblings of speculation within the Shadowers as to who was the better of the two.

"But if you'd like me to make her Trial *truly* difficult, I'll be happy to go grab the statue myself," Aahmes said, with a vicious grin for Namid. "Then we can see how well she does when she tries to steal something that's already been stolen once before. And recently."

More mutters followed that statement. Of course, anyone would increase their vigilance after someone had stolen something of theirs. And that would make any theft attempts that followed more than twice as difficult.

Namid shook her head. "The time is too short for such a task," she said, ignoring the suggestion he steal the Star first. "And with weapons-work thrown in…. I assume you want the weapons-work in the midst of all this?"

Aahmes nodded.

"As I expected," Namid said. "So, I say two nights beyond this to return with the Star. What say you?"

She had not yet accepted the test. The Shadowers watched, their intent expressions betraying their curiosity about what she had in mind.

"You're accepting?" Dar said, his voice incredulous.

Namid held up a hand, asking for silence. "Would you give me this long?" she said to Aahmes.

Aahmes peered at her, with a look like he was trying to decipher her intentions. Then he shrugged and his expression changed to a lazy, infuriating grin. "Why not?"

Namid raised her voice to carry over the mutters that started up again. "In that case, hear my idea for an alteration to the terms of the Trial. I'll agree to get the Star of Corentris before the third dawn hence, if…."

She paused a breath-of-time for effect, then continued, "If Aahmes agrees to return it afterward."

"Return it?" someone shouted from her right, over the sudden din.

"Yes, return it," Jaikrein shouted back. "We all know it can't be kept from its owner longer than half a day without him learnin' its exact location. And then he'd be comin' for it! D'you want an angry mage stormin' in here after his pretty statue?"

Dar shot Namid a look that told her he thought this was madness. But, after she indicated that she wanted to speak, he called for silence. This time, however, whispers and rustles continued in the background.

"That's my counter," Namid said. "If my *most worthy* Trial overseer accepts my conditions, then I accept his test." She gave Aahmes a mock bow, putting all the derision she could into the gesture.

Aahmes frowned at her, studying her. Then his gaze flicked around the room and he nodded. "I agree to this. By the third dawn from now, you'll put the Star of Corentris into my hands."

"Agreed," Namid said, sealing the terms of her Trial.

The room again exploded into a confusion of voices and this time they would not be silenced. The Shadowers who knew Namid well crowded around to offer their good wishes.

Aahmes fought his way through the crowd and leaned close. "I agreed only because I know I'll not be called on to return the Star," he told her in a quiet voice.

Namid gave him a tranquil look. "We'll see," she said.

"Yes, we shall see," he said. "And you'll face me tomorrow after the evening meal for the weapons-work part of your Trial." He laughed as he walked away.

Perhaps a quarter candle-mark after Aahmes left, and after the other Shadowers had finally returned to their own pursuits, Namid took a seat against the wall to nurse a drink and try to plan how she would accomplish this task.

To her surprise, a Shadower she had seen periodically around Shadow Keep, but did not know, took that moment to join her.

Namid stared at the short, lanky man with his crooked nose and scraggly, pale yellow hair and whiskers. What could he possibly want? After a breath-of-time, she remembered his name: Macai.

They had not encountered each other often, although she knew of him. He was known in the Shadowers for his love of elaborate schemes to accomplish the simplest of things. His schemes, deceptions within deceptions, rarely worked out as he intended. And they usually ended with him attracting the attention of the City Warders.

Namid gave him a questioning look.

"Well, young Shadower, you've got yourself a task worthy of the name 'Trial'," he said with a grin. "I have some helpful ideas to share with you…."

And he launched into a lengthy, convoluted explanation of what she should do, detailing the plans for some elaborate plot for her to get the statue.

She stopped listening almost immediately and let her thoughts drift, trying to think of possibilities that might actually work. She had finished her drink, even just taking a sip of it at a time, before Macai reached the end of his plan.

"And finally, if you can get the spiny-ray fish—you

really must get the fish, the blue spiny-ray, if you can—that will make the entire thing worthwhile," he concluded.

"Fish?" Had he heard somehow about what she had done to free Orran and Zwena?

Jaikrein joined them then and interrupted whatever answer Macai had with a hand on the lanky man's shoulder.

"Ah, Macai, now you're knowin' how these things go," Jaikrein said, giving the man's shoulder a squeeze. "Our Namid's got to be doin' this one on her very own."

"Oh, aye, right you are." Macai rose quickly and scurried off. He glanced back at Namid and mouthed the words, "Remember the fish," as he joined a group of Shadowers several tables away.

Sighing to herself, Namid rose too, to get more to drink, and found Jaikrein right next to her.

The older woman pulled her into a hug and pounded her on the back. In a raised voice, she wished her luck and warned her to watch out for Aahmes. Then she whispered in Namid's ear.

"Word about town is Chendrukhar's plannin' some kind of gatherin' for three nights from now. Of course, that'll be too late to be of any use...."

A last pat on her back and Jaikrein walked away, turning once to wink over her shoulder at Namid.

CHAPTER 5

Later that night, Namid sat alone in the hall, at last empty of all the excited Shadowers. She was on her own now. No other Shadower could help her in this. By giving her the bit of information that she had, Jaikrein had skirted close to breaking that rule. But Namid was glad that she had. That bit might prove important and useful.

Namid cradled her head in her hands and stared at the scarred tabletop. As an apprentice, she had heard many times from the experienced Shadowers how a party made a good distraction. But it was no help when it was a day too late. Now, if that could be changed….

Namid grimaced. She saw no way that the mage would change his plans because she wanted him to, even if she asked him. She chuckled at the image of presenting herself at his door and asking, as polite as could be, if he would please hold his party one day earlier.

She shook her head, dismissing her fanciful imagining.

So, what might cause him to change the date? She straightened as an idea came to her. If an important guest, for some reason, needed to leave early…. Maybe the guest of honor… if the gathering *was* in someone's honor.

Namid jumped up with her first step in mind. She had to find out who would be attending that gathering.

As she ran to her room to get more of her coins—in case she might need them—and her cloak, Namid's thoughts whirled through the possibilities. What would persuade a guest to leave early? But not too early? Namid had already decided that the best time for the party, for her purposes, would be the last night of her Trial. This would allow her the most preparation time. A tragedy in the family? No. No guest would want to stay for a party under those circumstances. The guest would want to leave right away.

It needed to be something that required timing, something to get a guest to leave no earlier or later than the morning after her Trial ended. The reason would have to depend on the guest she chose to use, which put her right back to her need to know who would be there.

Namid slipped out of the Keep, her cloak pulled tight against the late winter chill. The streets were gloomy, the normal state of affairs, but her eyes adjusted to the murk in just a few short breaths-of-time. She turned left and headed off to find Kaelior, a warrior a few years older than Namid, who often worked for the City Warders as one of the peacekeepers in Rhadanthus. Namid knew Kaelior frequented The Cup tavern when not on duty with the Warders, so she decided to look for her there first.

Luck was with her – she caught Kaelior at the door as the tall warrior was leaving to walk her rounds. Kaelior invited Namid to join her.

As they walked, the warrior glanced at Namid.

"So, you now walk weaponless?" Kaelior said, patting her sword sheathed at her side.

Namid laughed. "I just don't like to be obvious."

Kaelior studied Namid's gray-clad form, almost invisible in the night. "You're succeeding. Now what can I do for you? Much as I might wish otherwise, you didn't just seek me out for company for a nighttime stroll."

"Yeah, true," Namid said. "I'm interested in a party."

"Party person? Or party celebration?"

"Celebration. Given by Chendrukhar."

Kaelior gave a soft whistle. "Tough game. Planning to attend?" She grinned at Namid, her head canted a little to the left, a thing she did when feeling whimsical. Several strands of her light brown hair slid across her brown eyes, but she ignored them.

Namid shook her head. "Not exactly. I need to know who's invited, and the inns where they're staying."

Kaelior stopped and her smile disappeared. "What are you involved in now?"

Namid studied her, debating how much to say. While a friend—at least as much of one as anyone found in this city—Kaelior did still serve in the City Warders.

"It's my Trial," Namid said after a short breath-of-time. "Can you do this for me?"

Kaelior started walking again. "So, you decided to join up with that group of rogues, after all."

"Better than a lot of the alternatives," Namid said.

Kaelior nodded. "I'll grant you that."

After some silent consideration, she continued. "I suppose I can get the information for you. When do you need it?"

"As soon as possible. Dawn? Can you do it?"

Kaelior nodded again. "Think so. Where'll I meet you?"

"The Cup, of course. And wait for me if I'm a little late. Say, are any of the trader caravans in the city yet?"

"Just Milda's, so far. She's the first to brave the weather, as usual. I think she plans to head back out at the end of the week."

"Milda?" Namid repeated, with a smile. "I should've guessed that she'd be here already. This is good. Know where she's staying?"

"Her usual haunt, I'd guess."

Namid grinned. "Good. See you at dawn." She started

to move off, but Kaelior grabbed her arm.

Namid turned slowly, giving Kaelior a quizzical look. The warrior might be the closest thing to a friend she had among non-Shadowers in the city, but still, a wise resident never took anyone's motives for granted. Too often, people found friendship fleeting in Rhadanthus.

At the look on Namid's face, Kaelior released her and backed up a step. "Just wanted to tell you to be careful."

Namid relaxed. "Aren't I always?" she said with a slight smile. She slipped away into the darkness without giving Kaelior a chance to answer.

Namid used shortcuts through the city that she had discovered over the previous couple of years and, several long breaths-of-time later, stood in the shadows across from the Wayfarers Inn, a place frequented by the more successful merchants and traders who came to the city. Several torches on the front of the building lit the open yard where caravans frequently unloaded. That time of night, and this early in the trading season, the yard stood empty, any wagons and horses safely tucked away in nearby stables.

Namid frowned at the brightness and pulled her long cloak around her to hide her ragged clothes as much as possible. Maybe she should have stopped back at the Keep for some better clothes…. After some consideration, she pulled up her hood, too.

She stepped through the door, trying to project a sense that she belonged there, and gasped as the noise of the busy common room and the smells of numerous exotic drugs and drinks assaulted her nose. She held her breath the best she could and made her way to the bar to shout in the tender's ear. He pointed to the stairway and held up three fingers.

In the quieter hallway of the second floor, Namid located room number three, and knocked.

After some grumbling from the other side of the door, it swung open a crack. A large man who smelled of wine, and other things, looked out.

"Waddya want?"

"I need to speak with Milda."

The man glanced back into the room, then gave Namid a glare as he stepped back to let her pass, leaving the door open. Namid entered and kept an eye on the man while she tried at the same time to look all around for any threats. He closed the door behind her.

Further back in the room, a small lantern cast dim light on a woman more delicate-looking than Namid, older by over a score of years, and with lighter skin and nondescript brown hair. She beckoned Namid closer. "You wanted to see me?"

Namid nodded. "Can we talk alone?"

Milda looked her over—what she could see of her anyway—then shrugged. "You heard her, boys. Scram."

Namid waited until the last of Milda's men had gone— a couple of them out the door toward other parts of the inn and the rest just into another room—then pushed back her hood.

"I've got a favor to ask."

Milda grinned in delight. "Namid! Sit down, child. Well, not a child anymore, are you. Never expected to find you in this dump of a city. So, you decided to leave those Praznies after all?"

Namid shrugged. "Got tired of traveling all the time," she said.

Milda laughed. "Can't see that myself. Love the freedom to pack up and move on when I tire of a place. But have a drink. And what is this favor that you would ask?"

"No drink, thanks, Milda. I can't stay long. The favor I'd ask is, when you head back out, might you be able to change your schedule? Move it up so that you can leave three days from now, or so? And also possibly change your destination, depending on where you're currently planning to go next?

Milda gave her a shrewd look and sipped from her glass, studying Namid's serious demeanor. "Possibly. Why?"

Namid gave her a tight smile. "You're not supposed to be asking that question in Rhadanthus, you know. Can we just say that I believe an important person will have the need to leave three days from now, and just might want to travel with a caravan? No reason it couldn't be yours."

"An important person, huh?" From Milda's expression, Namid thought she must be considering the potential for profit. "Who?"

"I don't know, yet. But as soon as I do, so will you."

Milda nodded. "I suppose I can always let your important person persuade me to change my schedule and direction…."

"Monetarily, of course."

"Of cour—"

An insistent pounding on the door interrupted her. One of Milda's men stalked in from the other room and opened the outer door a crack. He spoke to someone outside, then turned to the two women.

"City Warders," he reported. "They demand we hand over the Shadower that's here."

CHAPTER 6

Cold fear washed over Namid. Not counting Kaelior, and perhaps a few others, the Warders as a group tended to act hostile to all Shadowers, whether they caught them stealing, or just caught them. Most Warders took any opportunity to grab any Shadowers they could, just on principle. The Shadowers *were* known as a guild of thieves, after all.

"Shadower?" Milda mouthed the word, as she moved toward the door while giving Namid a speculative look. Namid tried to give her a nonchalant smile, but it came out more a grimace.

How could the Warders have known a Shadower was here? Namid thought no one in the common room would have recognized her for what she was. Her nondescript cloak—something any non-noble might wear in Rhadanthus—should not have been marked as out of place.

If the Warders caught her, they'd chain her, haul her off to lock her up somewhere….

She couldn't face that. Not again!

Namid fought her rising panic, tried to still her shaking

hands. She spun around and scanned the room for inspiration. She could hide. Maybe under the bed? No, too obvious. In the chest? Yeah, right. Under the small table? Might as well just perch on top of it for all the concealment it offered. She doubted the adjoining room held any better options.

Maybe she could bluff her way out of this. She did not look like the typical Shadower... but she also did not look like she belonged in a quality inn such as this one, dressed as she was—other than her cloak—in clothes not much better than rags. And dragging Milda further into this would be a poor way to repay her friendship, anyway.

As she worked to think of something, she half-listened to Milda talking with the Warders, stalling them. How *could* they have known to find her here? She clenched her fists and stared off into the distance, fighting to get her thoughts in order.... And realized she was staring at the room's single window.

She dashed to it and threw open the shutters. The second-floor window opened on a narrow alley that ran behind the inn. Namid saw no sign of any Warders. She took a deep breath, fighting for calm.

Not that it worked.

How to get down? Just jumping was not an option. If she did that, she would probably break something on the cobblestones below. She leaned out the window and spotted a ledge that might save her.

She turned back to let Milda know her plan. But the trader seemed to have already figured it out and waved at her to go, using one hand hidden from the Warders by the door she held still mostly closed.

So Namid slipped through the window and closed its shutters behind her without a sound, while she teetered on the narrow ledge that circled the inn between the first-story and second-story windows. She held her breath for a few breaths-of-time, listening. She could hear the Warders in Milda's room. It sounded like three of them. It would not be long before they checked the window.

As fast as she dared, Namid edged along the ledge until she rounded a corner of the inn. She spotted a heap of trash beneath her. Another deep breath to steady herself, a quick entreaty to any gods who might care, and she jumped.

Not the most pleasant of landings, she mused as she tried to brush off the muck. But at least better than lying broken on the hard cobblestones. As she hurried away from the inn, she wondered, yet again, how they had found her there. And why? Kaelior had known....

A horrible suspicion settled in the pit of her stomach. She glanced at the sky, noting by the stars that she had some time until dawn. But dawn or not, she decided she needed to find Kaelior, needed to get an explanation from the warrior.

The light breeze that flowed almost constantly through the city changed direction, swirling around her in the narrow alley, and she caught a whiff of herself. She wrinkled her nose as she resisted the urge to gag.

Kaelior could wait, she decided. First, she had to get rid of that stench. Her ability to move about unnoticed would not do her any good if everyone could smell her.

She turned aside at the next crossroad and headed for Carssi's Baths a few streets over. She assumed they would still be taking customers so late.

As she approached the front of the building, she smiled. Considering the variety of diversions offered there, there had been little chance that she would have found it closed.

Inside the entrance, the pretty boy there frowned at her and pinched his nose against the smell that came from her clothes. He insisted on seeing her money first.

Namid protested at first, but when they started to attract attention, she handed over the entire amount and requested a bath alone. She made it clear that she was interested only in cleaning up and had *no* desire for companionship of any sort.

The boy tried to look disappointed—and failed—as he explained that all bath pools were in use. However, they did have some bathing shifts, if she would be willing to share the water with some other disinterested person. From his expression, she guessed that he hoped she would just decide to leave.

Instead she agreed, her voice betraying her irritation, and snatched the short, thin shift he offered her.

"My clothes need to be clean by the time I'm ready to leave. Which will be very soon," Namid told the boy as she stalked toward the changing room.

When she emerged from the small room, clad in the sleeveless shift that only reached to her knees, a girl about the same age as the boy at the door directed her to the correct pool. Namid kept her right arm tucked close to her side as she walked, to hide the small tattoo on her wrist. If anyone were to recognize the mark, it would raise too many questions that she did not want to answer.

From behind the various screens she passed, Namid heard some laughter and murmurs from other customers. But most sounds were hidden by the music that Carssi's minstrels played as they strolled along the paths between pools. The scents from the various herbal extracts that Carssi liked to add to the pool waters mingled in the air. Namid hoped the pool she would use did not have a heavily scented extract. That would cause her just as much trouble as if she left the stink alone.

Her pool sat near two other pools, both of which were full of lounging people who talked and laughed together. The water in her pool looked murky with the added extracts, concealing anything beneath the surface, but she smelled no overwhelming scent. Should be good enough.

Then she pulled up short. Her pool was unoccupied except for one young man who reclined in the water, submerged to his shoulders, sipping a glass of wine. She knew his shaggy dark hair and sharp features all too well.

He looked up and grinned, raising the glass to her in greeting.

"Well met, Namid. I see you got away." He spoke loud enough for her to hear, but not so loud that the others in the other pools could. He wrinkled his nose as she approached. "And I can see—or smell, rather—why you've decided to stop in here. Although time's passing."

"Aahmes, you...." She stopped for lack of the proper term for him, and instead snatched a small cleaning cloth and tiny piece of soap from a nearby bench. She slipped into the pool, as far away from him as she could get.

"*You* sent the Warders after me, didn't you?" She kept her voice as quiet as his had been. She began to scrub with the soap and cloth, planning to spend as little time there as possible.

"I, my dear young tyro?" He shrugged and shifted along the side of the pool so her soapy water ran past him to the outlet. "All I know is that they received word that someone they might be interested in had been seen lurking about that inn. Someone who was part of that Inner Ring affair more than a winter ago."

"You know as well as I who was really neck deep in that mess." She gave him a pointed look.

Aahmes shrugged. "I can't imagine what you're talking about."

He took a sip of his wine. "You must be so proud of yourself, having already worked out exactly how to accomplish your task so you can take time to linger here and wash up," he said. "What's next? A visit to one of those fancy-dress shops to get yourself a pretty gown? Maybe you'd better wait until after you've failed your Trial and see if you can get a new gown in your new position as some lady's assistant. Or, no, server in some tavern, more likely."

Namid glared at him, then turned her back on his laughter and tried to hurry through the rest of her bath, tried to ignore how her skin prickled with her awareness of his gaze.

But when she glanced back, he was not looking at her at all. Rather, he leaned back with both arms stretched out to the sides along the rim of the pool, head tilted back, with a slight smile on his lips. It looked like his eyes were closed. Namid resisted the sudden urge to soak him with a large splash.

A quick sniff of her arm and hair told her she had managed to wash away the stench. The slight stream of water that circulated through the pool had already taken away the soapy dirt she had washed off and she found the pool's pleasant temperature inviting. She would have enjoyed resting in the warm water, but she stood to go, cutting short her stay.

"I'll finish some other time. When they've cleared the waters of *all* the scum," she tossed back over her shoulder at Aahmes.

He laughed as she stalked off.

She returned to the changing room and found her clothes waiting. They were still damp, but at least no noxious odor wafted from them.

Namid breathed easier when she returned to the darkness of the streets, then shivered in the chill air. Damp clothes and wet hair did not make for a comfortable walk in the late-winter night.

She decided to wait until dawn to speak with Kaelior, as they had agreed. After that little exchange with Aahmes, she believed that he alone was behind the business at Milda's inn.

CHAPTER 7

Namid jogged toward the East Gate, her steps quiet even as she moved quickly, trying to stay warm in the cold darkness. She fought the fatigue that was creeping up on her and hoped the guard at the gate was someone she knew. She wanted to take a look at Chendrukhar's home, if she could.

The man at the East Gate was not the one Namid had hoped to see there. But for a few korz, and the promise of a few more when she returned, he let her out and agreed to let her back in when she knocked.

After she stepped through, he closed the gate behind her, leaving her alone in the night outside the wall of Rhadanthus. Only one of the five moons hung in the sky, but the stars provided more light than they did within the city.

From the city gate, Namid could make out the dark bulk of Chendrukhar's imposing stronghold some distance away. She walked toward it, just one more patch of shadow in the darkness. She stopped ten paces or more from the structure and circled it at a slow walk.

Three tall towers connected by bridges at various levels

comprised Chendrukhar's hold. Namid estimated the tallest tower to be close to thirty paces high, with the other towers each perhaps as much as ten paces shorter. A stone wall four or so paces tall surrounded the towers, broken only by a double gate. Namid walked up to the wall and discovered its stones were almost as tall as she was. They felt as smooth as glass and fit so closely together that she had trouble both seeing and feeling the edges where each of the stones touched the next.

She would not be climbing that.

Two squat towers incorporated into the wall flanked the gate and reached above the wall about a pace. The ironbound gate reached nearly as high as the wall. In the night, everything about the hold looked gray and black, but Namid knew the stones showed a blue tint in the daylight. And, when seen in sunlight, the color of the wood of the double gate nearly matched the stones.

Namid heard faint rustling sounds from the other side of the gate and wall, but saw no light, or sign of life. She spent much of the remainder of the night studying the mage's hold and the land around it as well as she could.

Sunrise found her on a low bench by the door of The Cup, waiting for Kaelior while struggling to stay awake. After she got the names from the warrior, she needed to find someplace quiet to sleep a little.

But she had promised to tell Milda... but first she would have to compose a message for the guest.... Namid dropped her head to her hands and tried to silence her thoughts.

Someone grabbed her shoulder.

Namid jumped and twisted away with a stiletto held ready in each hand. Then she finished waking up and realized that it was Kaelior.

She smiled at the warrior's expression and returned her blades to their sheaths within the two leather armguards she wore. Avoiding any sudden movements, Kaelior held out a sheet of paper.

"Sorry I'm late," she said. "I didn't mean to frighten you."

"No apology needed. And you didn't," Namid assured her and took the paper. "But I'm afraid that I, at least, alarmed you. Now, let's see what we have here. Hmm, quite an impressive guest list he has. Are these all of them?" Namid deliberately chattered to give Kaelior time to regain her composure.

"All that I could find out about." Kaelior studied Namid for a breath-of-time. "I didn't realize you were so fast…."

"Why do you think Shadowers are so difficult to catch?" Namid said with a grin.

A name on the list caught Namid's eye. "Lady Livian of Tige, huh? Isn't she still in the middle of that struggle for those vineyards near the capital city, along the western shore of Lake Kundu?" She stared off into the distance and pictured a map of that part of Paronia, central of the Six Realms. "Yes… and her only real opponent is Lord Edmer of Tun-Lir, who holds the rest of the shoreline there. I think she'll do."

"You seem to know a lot about what's going on outside Rhadanthus," Kaelior said. "I've never before heard of either of those people."

Namid smiled. "I listen," was all she said by way of explanation.

She had already known something of the nobles and their situation from her time before Rhadanthus, when she had lived in the capital of the Six Realms. Since then, she had heard a few new tidbits when skulking about the wealthier portions of Rhadanthus. But she had no intention of letting anyone know exactly how she knew such things, not even Kaelior.

"My thanks for the list," Namid said. "Oh, and perhaps you'd better forget about this. It might get a bit tight."

Kaelior gave her a long, searching look. "Don't you go too far," she said. "I'd hate to have to lock you up."

Namid nodded, with a slight smile. "I'd hate that, too." She yawned.

Kaelior grinned. "Looks like someone better get some sleep." Then she yawned, too. "Maybe two someones. If you need someplace out of the way to catch a few candle-marks' sleep, I've got a house that's not too far from here. My daughter stays there."

"That sounds perfect," Namid said. "Which way?"

"I'll take you." Kaelior headed down the street. Namid jogged a few steps to catch her.

"I didn't know you had a daughter."

Kaelior chuckled. "We haven't exactly shared family stories, have we?"

"No," Namid said with a smile.

"My brother stays with her when I'm on Warder duty. She follows him around like she's his shadow, really. He's teaching her how to bake, so maybe she'll follow in his footsteps. Feed people, instead of fight them."

"Sounds nice," Namid said and stifled another yawn.

"Stop that," Kaelior grinned as she also tried to stifle a yawn. "It'd be nicer somewhere else, I've been thinking. Get us all away from this city. Not a place to raise a kid."

"Mhm," Namid said. "Probably right." She yawned again.

Kaelior nodded. And yawned, too. "Better get home before we both fall over asleep right here in the street."

Less than a quarter candle-mark brought them to a neat little house at the edge of one of the better parts of the city. Kaelior introduced Namid to her brother, a young man about Namid's age, and to her daughter, a quiet little girl of about five.

Namid murmured something polite and was relieved when they showed her to a bed in a back room. She kicked off her boots and stretched out, asleep almost before she could pull up the covers.

~ ~ ~

Bright light in the room woke Namid. She rolled off the bed and padded to the window. By the height of the sun, she judged that it was somewhat past midday. She pulled on her boots, waved goodbye to Kaelior's daughter and brother—they barely noticed her as they worked on some baked goods in the kitchen—and headed back toward Shadow Keep.

Namid's thoughts returned to the pieces she was trying to manipulate to succeed at her Trial. Lady Livian would work for what she planned, she decided as she walked. And Namid had heard rumors that the lady and Chendrukhar were close friends, perhaps even more than friends.

Now, what to say in the letter that would take the Lady of Tige away earlier than she had planned? It should be from her brother, Lord Saward, Namid decided.

Then she realized that she would need parchment and a good quill, neither of which she could find at Shadow Keep. She shook her pouch and decided that she had enough with her. She located the proper shop and purchased one sheet of the finest parchment she could afford and a nice, new quill. Dar's ink would do.

However, she realized that she would also need to somehow duplicate the seal of Lord Saward of Tige. She tried to think of a way to do it herself, but when no reasonable ideas came to her, she had to admit that she would need to get a copy from Falgien. Although she disliked him, she knew he would do an excellent job.

On the way to Falgien's place, Namid's stomach growled, several times. Since she had to pass near Shadow Keep anyway, she decided to grab something from the kitchen there. But on her way through the Keep, she realized she needed to get a few things from her room, so she turned aside to visit there first.

In her room, she retrieved the last of her coins from hiding, including her one navn. Falgien's work was good...

and expensive, especially if he needed to be hurried along. She hoped she would not have to give him *all* her coins.

While in her room, she hauled out the best of her clothes and changed into them. Although he often worked for the illicit elements of Rhadanthus, Falgien's shop sat in a better part of the city than the areas Namid usually frequented. Her best clothes, even plain and mismatched as they were, would let her pass in that ring as beneath the notice of the usual denizens, but not so far beneath as to—contrarily—be worthy of note.

After she finished dressing, she made a quick foray into the kitchen and returned with a small piece of meat atop a slice of fresh-baked bread. Then she headed for Falgien's place.

She had finished eating the food she brought with her before Falgien decided that he had time for her. He motioned her to a cushioned chair in his overcrowded, over-decorated workshop.

"Now, my sweet poppet, what is it that I can do for you?"

Namid reminded herself to ignore the more annoying aspects of his personality. "I need a copy of a seal. The one that belongs to Lord Saward of Tige."

"Simplicity itself, image of sweetness," Falgien beamed. "And it's my most profound pleasure to provide you with such a thing. I'll have it perfectly ready for you to pick up on the morrow, in the afternoon."

"I need it today."

"Today? Oh, the rush, the hard-hearted disregard for the time an artist needs to create true quality. Are you in such necessity, beauteous flower? Is it truly a matter of such urgency to you?"

"You might say that. I know you can have it ready."

"Of course. I could even hurry the work, sweet beauty. On any other, normal day. But this afternoon it's an impossibility. It just cannot be done. This is the afternoon that we, my whole family and I, celebrate my favorite cousin's glorious espousals. And I know you would never be so heartless as to see me miss it and cause her the disappointment of my absence as she celebrates the beginning of her new life."

Namid resisted the urge to sigh or take him by the shoulders and shake him. "Perhaps you could make the seal before you go," she said.

"Good idea, excellent idea!" His exaggerated expression of delight changed into an equally exaggerated mournful frown. "However, I have others who await my work most eagerly, and who came before you, my lovely."

"Perhaps… isn't it just possible… that you might have such a seal already prepared? Tucked away against some future need?" Namid shook her pouch, jingling the coins within.

"Ah, such an interesting question. It's possible that it might be so," Falgien admitted, eyeing her pouch. "I could conceivably have such an item safely stashed somewhere that would be what you need, joy of my eyes. But to even search, dear sweetness, would take more time than is available to me now."

"Perhaps I can offer an incentive. Something to make my order a higher priority." Namid held up her single navn, aware that he seldom received so much for only a single piece of his work. She watched eagerness slide across his expression as he eyed the gold coin. "This might also soothe your cousin if you are just the tiniest bit late to her celebration."

Falgien nodded several times. "Indeed, I can see that it just might do that. Return in two candle-marks, precious flower, and I will have your seal." He reached for the coin, but Namid pulled it back.

"When I get my seal," she said.

"Of course, of course. Now, hurry off. Take yourself off to wherever it is you go when you are not lighting my shop with your presence, distracting me and interrupting my work…."

Namid gave him a sweet, false smile. "Certainly. Don't let me keep you any longer."

Back outside the shop, Namid took a couple of deep breaths to ease the tension that gripped her whenever she dealt with Falgien. That had been much easier, and had also cost less, than she had feared.

CHAPTER 8

Back in Shadow Keep, Namid borrowed Dar's desk for a brief time, with his permission. There she wrote a letter addressed to Lady Livian of Tige from her brother Lord Saward.

The letter informed Livian that in two weeks' time, Lord Edmer had an audience with their overlord, during which he would claim that the Lady no longer had any interest in the vineyards. Livian would need to leave Rhadanthus no later than the second morning after receiving the letter—the morning before Chendrukhar's planned celebration—to arrive in front of their overlord during Edmer's audience. Unfortunate, but necessary. And Livian must be certain to leave no earlier or later, as her arrival would be most effective if she entered *during* the audience.

Namid signed Lord Saward's name, then paused. By custom, scribes who wrote letters for the nobility left their own small signatures at the bottom of those letters. Namid had no idea who Saward's scribes might be and, after some thought, decided that Livian would likely not know either, not all of them anyway. So, she made up something that sounded like a name and signed it at the bottom.

Namid folded the parchment with extreme care and took it to her room, where she hid the letter in a niche that she alone knew about. Then she pawed through the clothes she had left scattered about. By city requirement, those who ran messages in Rhadanthus all wore clothing that matched in color, even if threadbare. As she suspected, none of her clothing would do to present herself as a respectable, but poor, messenger.

She ran downstairs to Keizha's underground rooms, located just below the Keep's main level and next to the large room that sometime in the past had been used to house all the apprentices. The only Shadower to have two rooms, Keizha only used about half of one of them for herself. The rest of that one, and her other room, held a great variety of things the Shadowers might need to use for a guise on a job. Anything the Shadowers picked up that they decided was not valuable enough to sell right away came to Keizha for later use.

The tiny woman—her head just topped Namid's shoulder—opened her door with a smile when Namid knocked. None of the Shadowers seemed to know just how old, or young, Keizha might be. Keizha's chin-length white hair, caught back behind her ears, implied age. But her smooth golden-brown skin and dark, dark eyes made her seem little older than Namid. But Namid felt certain that Keizha *was* older than her.

"Thought I'd be seeing you at my door before oh-too-long," Keizha greeted Namid and pulled the younger woman inside. Keizha tucked a few unruly strands of hair back behind her ears as she closed the door.

"So, what is it you're needin'?" she said. "Oh, and congratulations on the startin' of your Trial."

"My thanks," Namid said. "I need to be a messenger, poor but trustworthy."

Keizha nodded and circled Namid, looking her over.

"Yah, you can carry it off," she said. "Plannin' t' go as a

girl or boy?"

Namid gave that some thought. She had not considered that aspect earlier.

"Boy, I think," she said after a breath-of-time.

Keizha nodded and waved a hand toward some shelves in a corner. "Take a look. You should be findin' what you need in what's there."

Namid poked through the clothing on the shelves and found worn, but still intact outer- and under-tunics, trousers and a shirt, all in a dark blue. They matched each other well enough to pass as a messenger's garb. After some hunting around, she found a cap that matched well enough, too, and would hold and hide her hair. On a bottom shelf, she found a dark blue cloak, shorter than she would have liked, but the color matched the rest of the clothes… and it would be warm enough and had a hood, should she need it. Her own boots would do, worn and scuffed, but good enough for her guise.

She turned to let Keizha know she had what she needed and jumped, startled to find the woman right behind her. Keizha chuckled at her expression.

"Before I settled into these rooms and took over seein' to all this, I was the best of us," Keizha said. "Of course, that was oh-so-many years ago. Even taught young Dar a thing or two." She winked at Namid.

Keizha pulled a long strip of brown cloth off a mismatched pile of cloth on a nearby table and held it out to Namid.

"You'll be wantin' this, too, my dear."

She chuckled at Namid's blank look and waved a hand toward the younger woman's chest. "You've got just enough curves there that you'll be needin' to bind them if you're wantin' to pass as a boy."

Namid glanced down. "Oh. Right."

She gave Keizha a slight smile, abashed, as she took the strip of cloth and gathered up the clothing she had selected. "My thanks."

"Good luck to you," Keizha said. "You show up that too-full-of-himself young man. And bring everythin' back when you're done with it all.'"

Namid nodded agreement then ran back to her room — she seemed to be doing a lot of running of late. Since she still had some time before she was due to meet Falgien, she decided to return to Milda. She dressed in her messenger-guise clothes and, for the moment, tucked the cap in her belt. She could feel cold flowing in from the one wall of her room that was part of Shadow Keep's outer wall, so she wrapped up in the short blue cloak.

Outside the Wayfarers Inn, Namid stuffed her hair into her cap before entering, leaving the hood of her cloak down this time. Several strands of her too-long bangs escaped the confining cap and hung partially over one eye. She frowned, but decided they would be fine like that and just pulled the cap a little lower on her forehead.

Namid found Milda in the common room and, acting her role of messenger, waited in discreet silence to one side until Milda noticed her. When the trader waved to her to approach, her eyes widening as she recognized her, Namid whispered her message that Lady Livian of Tige would be the person Milda would be dealing with. Milda nodded her understanding and pressed a coin into Namid's hand to help support her messenger guise. Namid gave a clumsy bow of thanks and hurried out. She headed then to Falgien's, tucking her hat in her belt again as she walked.

Falgien waited for her, already dressed in fancy clothes for his cousin's espousals. Through the front window of his shop, Namid saw him pacing.

When she stepped inside, he bowed to her with an exaggerated flourish and presented her with a small ring, of a size that might fit a man's smallest finger. Namid examined it and found no flaws. Although he kept shifting in impatience, Falgien took the time to let her try it out with some sealing wax. She studied the resulting impression.

"The rendition is completely accurate, sweet blossom," Falgien assured her. "The best, of course, for you."

"Very nice." She handed him the promised payment. "I'll certainly recommend your work."

He bowed, thanking her in elaborate terms, praising her discernment and generosity, then ushered her out the door, almost pushing her in his eagerness to have her gone.

Namid returned to Shadow Keep and retrieved the letter from her room. She found a candle in the kitchen, dripped some of the wax on the letter and pressed the ring into it. From the activity around her in the kitchen, Namid knew the evening meal would soon be ready. She decided to stay for it. She wanted to deliver the letter after dark anyway.

Back in her room, she hid the letter again. She also changed out of her messenger guise before she joined the others in the hall. She surprised herself by refilling her plate, and felt pleasantly full afterward, but not overly so. Her table companions asked pointed questions about her progress on her Trial, to which she gave vague replies.

She once caught Aahmes watching her and gave him a wide grin. Let him wonder at it. Her plans were settling into place as well as she could hope. Except, perhaps, for finding the Star in the mage's hold.

The layout of those towers of Chendrukhar's concerned her. The Star could be anywhere in there, but she knew of no one, other than the mage himself, who would be able to tell her where she could find it. And she had no intention of trying to get that information from *him*. That would be folly. Worse than folly, even.

After the meal ended, the Shadowers moved the tables aside. When Namid realized why, she wished she had not eaten so much.

How could she have forgotten that it was time for the weapons-work portion of her Trial?

CHAPTER 9

Namid moved out of the way so the Shadowers could finish clearing an open space in the center of the room. She looked around but could not spot Aahmes. Might he have forgotten, too?

Somehow, she doubted it.

Namid began working through some warm-up moves the Shadowers taught, trying to work the cold out of her muscles before the bout. Jaikrein positioned herself close, leaning against the wall to watch her.

"Watch yourself against Aahmes," she said after a few breaths-of-time, gesturing to where the younger Shadower now stood across the room. "I don't like the look he's got in his eyes."

"Oh?" Namid said.

"Aye, take a look."

Namid paused and studied Aahmes. As she watched, he whirled through a string of mock attacks at speed, clearing a space around himself. Then he looked at her.

She shuddered. He looked so serious, grim even. Could she have been mistaken earlier? *Was* he out to kill her?

He gave her a mocking bow and turned his back.

No, she would not believe that. This bout was not a deathmatch, after all. But the sliver of fear that wormed its way through her warned her that in all likelihood he would try to take her out in such a way that she could not complete the thievery portion of the Trial.

Not only a possibility, but nearly a certainty, she decided.

She tried to push the fear away, but after seeing those mock attacks, she wondered if she was good enough to keep him from doing it. The fear settled into a knot inside her, right about where her evening meal sat. And a sliver of doubt accompanied the fear. She had worked so hard for this. But was she good enough?

A touch on her arm brought her attention back to the room. "Namid? Are you, all right?"

She nodded and smiled at Jaikrein's concern. "Just trying to decide how I want to counter that." She waved a hand in Aahmes' general direction.

"You can still change your mind," Jaikrein said in a quiet voice. "Have one of the others test your weapons-work."

"No. It'll be fine."

Jaikrein gave her a look of disbelief, then shrugged. She pointed across the room, to three people standing less than two paces behind Aahmes, watching all the activity.

"Those three are your judges," Jaikrein said. "They'll be fair and also make sure Aahmes doesn't go too far."

If they can catch him in time, Namid added to herself. She had not heard of anyone being crippled from the weapons-work portion of their Trial, but there could always be a first time. Namid nodded to Jaikrein and studied the three. She did not know them well but knew something of them.

Thes, the man on the left with weathered skin and graying hair and beard, was older than Dar. He was seldom seen around the Keep. Word had it that he did 'special' tasks for Dar, and maybe also kept the elite of Rhadanthus from bothering the Shadowers, too much anyway. Thes was sometimes said to be of an age with Keizha, whatever age that was, and also was said to have been in the Shadowers about as long as Keizha.

The brown-haired, beige-skinned woman next to Thes was one of the weapons instructors of the Shadowers. Aerill was her name. From what Namid had heard, no weapon existed that Aerill could not use. Namid had learned a lot from Aerill during her apprenticeship.

The third person, Uffke—a thin man with short black hair and skin darker than Namid's—was another weapons instructor. Namid had worked with him some, but not as much as with Aerill. Uffke had been away much of the past year working on something with Thes, so the rumors said.

Namid performed a few more warm-up moves, then ran through a quick series of mock attacks against the air, much as Aahmes had done.

She heard murmurs from the gathered Shadowers and the clink of coins changing hands but tried to ignore it all. Her focus needed to be on Aahmes.

Dar stepped into the center of the room and everyone quieted. He carried a wooden box. He nodded to Aahmes and Namid, who both stepped out to stand in front of him. Dar opened the box.

"You'll start with one of these, a matching one for each of you."

Namid looked over the small selection of knives in the box. They all looked similar in quality, the lengths of their blades the only real variation.

With a sidelong look at Namid, Aahmes grabbed one of the two with the shortest blades. He held it out for her inspection. She considered it. With his longer reach, she would have to get in close. That would certainly test her skills.

She became aware of his intent look as he watched her. Could he guess what she was thinking? She shifted under his scrutiny and he grinned.

Namid nodded and grabbed the matching knife.

Dar set the box on the floor, near the edge of the cleared area.

"Leave your other blades with me," he instructed.

Namid had brought only a couple of hers with her. She watched, amused, as Aahmes divested himself of a variety of blades from various hiding spots about his person. When he finished, Dar held an impressive collection of knives.

Aahmes rolled up the sleeves of his tunic, baring forearms that carried scars from previous knife fights. Namid started to roll up her sleeves, then paused.

How could she have forgotten?

For this, she would be required to remove the leather armguards that she wore on each arm... but one covered that small tattoo. She needed to keep that hidden, needed to keep its import secret.

She plopped down on the floor and bent over to better hide her movements as she unlaced the armguards, making the activity more elaborate than necessary. As she removed the armguards, she pressed her thumb to the small tattoo and used the tiniest bit of her Power to hide the mark, making it blend in with the rest of her arm. Both the tattoo and her abilities with Power were secrets she had no intention of sharing, even with the Shadowers. The concealment would not last long, due to the nature of the tattoo, but should hold long enough for this.

Namid stood and handed the armguards to Dar, then stepped a pace or so away from Aahmes. Aahmes gave her an odd, unreadable look. She tilted her head and gave him a quizzical look with a slight smile.

Dar nodded and backed up to the edge of the cleared area, holding their personal weapons.

Thes stepped forward. "Both o' you know the rules for this. You can use anythin' you can get your hands on for a weapon, save only your own now in Dar's keepin'. The weapons-work Trial ends at first blood or when we three call it."

He stepped back and urged the watching Shadowers back as close to the walls as they could get.

Then he nodded to Aahmes and Namid to begin.

They both took knife-fighting stances and Aahmes attacked.

Namid managed to briefly trap his knife, but he caught her in a grapple. She kept him from slicing her but could not get free.

"You don't want to close with someone who's stronger than you," he murmured in her ear, then threw her back away from him.

She stumbled but managed to keep to her feet. She glared at him, fighting that fear, that sliver of doubt.

When he came for her again, right away, she scrambled to get away. And sudden anger washed away her fear and squelched the doubt.

Enough of this….

She had worked hard for this. She could do this – she *would* do this! Nothing—and no one—would keep her from her place in the Shadowers!

She found herself near the box of knives and grabbed a second blade. Taking a deep, steadying breath, she pursued Aahmes with a series of rapid attacks that kept him on the defensive.

None of her attacks got through.

Aahmes came back at her, faster than before, and nothing at all like the previous times they had sparred. He was not holding back at all on his attacks for this Trial.

She countered and avoided, with difficulty. And managed a slice toward his briefly exposed side.

She needed to be faster. She could do this.

Aahmes got away but nearly caught her with a slash of his own. From his attacks, she believed he meant to hurt her badly enough that she could not complete the rest of her Trial. With the Shadowers' inexperienced Healer, almost any serious wound made that a real possibility. She gave him a quick shake of her head and he laughed at her.

Namid lost her sense of the surrounding Shadowers, of their intent interest in the bout, even that they stood watching, except as obstacles to avoid.

There were only the blades and the wills behind them.

Faster....

Stab and slice. And she managed to keep Aahmes from getting to the box of knives.

A sudden clatter startled her. It sounded like someone had dropped some of the metal plates the Shadowers used at their meals.

Aahmes' eyes shifted the slightest bit to the side.

Namid lunged.

Entanglement and confusion and they both ended on the floor rolling away from each other, racing to be the first to stand again.

A shrill whistle tore through the room. The end signal.

Namid and Aahmes both stood but stayed where they were.

And pain shot through Namid's arm. She nearly dropped her knife. From a deep slash across her forearm, a thin stream of blood ran down and dripped off her fingers.

That was it, then.

She stared at the blood dripping on the floor and saw her hopes falling to the floor with it.

But then the whispers penetrated the gloom that had blanketed her. The clang of a knife as it hit the floor brought her head up.

Across from her, Aahmes clutched his bloody upper arm and glared at her. It looked like she had gotten him worse than he had gotten her.

She dropped to sit on the floor, feeling suddenly exhausted, and clamped her hand over her wound to try to slow the bleeding.

She had gotten Aahmes at the same time.

So, a draw. Not proof of who was better with knives

but, as Namid noted the nods from all three of the judges, good enough for her to pass the weapons-work part of the Trial.

She watched through gaps between the celebrating, exuberant Shadowers as Elnathan, their Healer, worked on Aahmes. She could somewhat sense the Power he used.

Elnathan was still new to using his Power to Heal but did manage stop the bleeding. Then he bound Aahmes' wound with a clean cloth and sent him off. The Healer came next to work on Namid's wound, treating it much the same way.

"I'm sorry I can't yet Heal completely," he said in a quiet voice as he finished. "That arm's going to be less use to you than normal for a while. Well beyond the end of your Trial, I'm afraid."

Namid nodded. "I expected as much. Still, you have my thanks."

He nodded and moved off, leaving Namid to the congratulations of the Shadowers.

Nearly a candle-mark later when she managed to get away, Namid headed to her room to try to sneak in a little rest. However, after tossing and turning for nearly half a candle-mark, she gave up and climbed out of bed. She dressed in her messenger guise again, and laced on her armguards beneath the shirt sleeves, hissing at the pain from the cut from Aahmes' knife. She tucked the letter she had written in her belt, put on the blue cloak, and slipped out.

CHAPTER 10

Until sundown, Namid perched on the city wall near the East Gate and stared toward Chendrukhar's hold. She hated the thought that she would have to go in there blind, but how was she to find out about the inside *before* going in after the Star?

When the sun slipped below the horizon, she climbed down from the wall, wincing at the pain from her injured arm. After a short search, she located a City Warder and asked directions—in her guise as a messenger—to the Lady Livian's residence in the city. Thanking the Warder, she then headed toward the house Livian had appropriated for herself for her stay in the city.

The house lay near the center of Rhadanthus, in the richer portion of the city. The streets seemed darker than usual and Namid appreciated that she saw so much better in the dark than most people.

As she walked, she tucked her hair into her cap. Without warning, she shivered, and wondered if it was going to snow. She then ran the rest of the way to Livian's door, so she would appear convincing. She pounded on the door several times. A servant opened it and looked down his nose at her.

She held out the letter. "Important letter fer th' Lady Livian," she panted. When the servant tried to take it, she told him, "Gotta give it to th' Lady herself."

The man scowled. "Follow me, boy."

He led her along a long hallway, up some stairs, and down another long hallway to a closed door. The servant knocked and a thin young woman in a simple yellow gown of fine linen opened the door. Her skin was darker than Namid's, and she wore her orange-brown hair in tight curls.

"This person claims he has an important message for you, my lady," the man told her.

The woman smiled and held out her hand for the letter. "I'm Livian. Is that it?"

Namid bowed and gave her the letter. "Aye, m'lady."

After a brief glance at the seal, Livian broke it, unfolded the parchment and read the contents. Namid watched in satisfaction as the lady first looked astonished, then angered, her eyebrows drawn down and a severe frown pulling at her lips.

When she finished reading, Livian ordered the servant to bring parchment and ink. She read the letter again, then seemed to remember Namid, and gave her a thoughtful look.

"Bad news, m'lady?" Namid said, giving her voice a deliberate tremor.

"In part, lad. Would you be willing to carry a letter for me?" She dug in her pouch and pulled out a navn. "I'll give you this for your trouble."

Namid acted awed and eager, the way she imagined a noble would expect a poor messenger to act when offered one of the gold coins. "Oh, aye, m'lady! Where'er you want me t' take it!"

"Good. Bide a few breaths-of-time, then."

Livian retreated into the room, followed by the servant, who had returned with parchment and ink. When Livian returned, she carried a sealed letter in her hand.

"What's your name, lad?" she said.

Name? Namid had not thought to come up with a name for herself in this guise. Then she almost smiled at the wicked thought that came to her. Why not?

"Aahmes, m'lady."

"Very well, Aahmes. I want you to deliver this for me tonight. And you must wait for a reply, if there is one. Can you read?"

Namid decided to stay safe. "No, m'lady."

"Excellent. Take this to the Lord Chendrukhar. Do you know who he is?"

Namid acted frightened. "Y-yes, m'lady. H-he'd be th' mage in th' hold outside th' w-walls."

Livian nodded and handed her the letter and the navn. Namid bowed and scurried away.

When she was sure she could not be seen from the house, Namid gave a skip of delight. What better way to get inside Chendrukhar's walls?

At the East Gate, Namid used the letter, and Lady Livian's name, to get through then hurried toward the mage's hold. Before she arrived at the double gate, a light snow started to fall. She shivered and broke into a jog to help keep warm and get there all the faster. She knocked twice on the gate before she got a response. The large gate swung open without a sound.

"What business have you here?" came a chill voice from the darkness.

Namid half-faked the tremor in her voice when she said that she had an important letter for the Lord Chendrukhar.

The echoing voice bade her enter and approach. The gate closed behind her with a solid thud. Namid noticed the air this side of the gate felt much warmer than that outside the walls.

Light flared from three widely spaced torches that hung on the walls, showing Namid a small courtyard in the dim, flickering light. In one corner, a deep shadow remained, which resolved itself into a tall man, robed in black, with skin lighter than Namid's.

In the minimal light, Namid saw the man's dark eyes glittering from beneath jutting brows. They framed a thin, sharp nose. His lips were thin, but his expression was not hostile. Wary, perhaps, or guarded. He was handsome, in an intimidating sort of way.

"Your name?" he said.

"A-Aahmes, sir… m'lord" Namid stammered, playing her role of unnerved messenger, although the unnerved part was more than half real.

"You have something for me."

"Aye." She hurried to him and slipped the parchment into his outstretched hand. She turned to leave, having decided she did not want to try to see the inside of the mage's home after all. And certainly not with him standing right there.

"Wait, Aahmes. If I need to reply, you can take that, too."

Right. Livian had also told her to wait for a possible reply.

So, Namid waited, standing more than a pace away from the mage and watching him. He took a step toward one of the torches then glanced at her and smiled. He held up one hand and two orbs of bright, golden light formed above his palm. They moved to float beside him, just above each of his shoulders. Namid made sure her expression showed fear and awe when he looked to see her reaction.

But when he started to read, she studied the yard around her and the light orbs. Her awe had been only mostly feigned; she had seen orbs of light similar to these before, but not so bright or clear. And she had not seen anyone form two at once.

From where she stood, Namid spotted a door set into a wall that ran from one of the shorter towers to the outer wall of the hold. A wall also connected the two shorter towers, blocking access to the taller tower, at least as far as she could tell. And she saw a single door leading into the second shorter tower.

When Chendrukhar finished reading, he stared off into the darkness for several long breaths-of-time. Then he looked at Namid again.

"Aahmes is not a girl's name," he said.

Namid stared in bewilderment. What did that have to do—? Oh.

"No, it's not," she said in a guarded tone. She looked at the ground, afraid of what he might read in her eyes. She jumped when he touched her cheek, so silently had he approached. His hand slid under her chin, lifted her head so he could look at her. She was surprised by how cool his hand felt.

"Why conceal yourself behind a boy's clothes and manners?"

Namid shrugged and surprised herself by answering. "You know what so many of the fortuneless in Rhadanthus do to be able to eat." She stepped away from him. "Is there a reply?"

He studied her a breath-of-time longer, then turned away. "Wait here."

He disappeared through the door Namid had spotted in one of the shorter towers, the light orbs following him, leaving her standing in the dim courtyard in the falling snow that melted as soon as it hit the stones underfoot. She looked around without moving from her spot. Nothing much to see. A lot of shadows from the flickering torches. The snow hissed when it hit the small flames.

This was her chance to look around more. But she stood frozen to the spot. He could be watching her.

He probably was.

She felt that someone, or something, watched her....

Namid spun. Did that shadow move? More than just from the flickering light? Another motion from the corner of her eye had her spinning the other way. What was there? She rubbed her arms to try to wipe away the prickling sense of being watched.

Hurry up, she silently urged the absent mage.

Chendrukhar returned about a quarter candle-mark later with a bundle of letters, which he handed to her. One light orb still followed him.

"Take these to the inns written on the outsides of them. You can read, can't you?"

Namid hesitated, remembering what she had told Lady Livian. "Yeah, I can read some," she said after a breath-of-time.

Not the whole truth, she reflected, but close enough for right then. He did not need to know more.

"Good. Get these there this night. Don't wait for replies. It's unlikely there will be any, anyway. This is for you." He dropped a small pouch, which jingled, into her hand.

"If you ever wish to be more than a messenger, you and I might be able to come to an arrangement."

"Oh?" Namid said and peered at him trying to read his expression.

Just what was he offering? She suspected his own version of the brothels in town.

"No, not that," he said, as if he knew her thoughts. "I can tell that you have the potential for a certain ability. I'm offering to teach you what you could learn about... Power."

She stared at him. So, he could sense that she had Power. But it seemed he could not tell that she already knew how to use it.

A generous offer to a chance-met messenger. And mages were typically not known for generosity.

She backed away and looked around like she sought an escape, working to give an impression of confusion and fear.

"I-I don't know...." She turned away.

The gate swung open before she reached it, allowing her to leave.

She ran.

She arrived at the city gate out of breath but able to laugh to herself at the guard's wary expression. The manner of her return would add to Chendrukhar's already formidable reputation in Rhadanthus. She fled down the street before the guard could ask her story.

Several streets away from the gate, Namid stopped in the dim light near one of the few lit street-lanterns. She read the names of the inns on the letters and whistled to herself. They represented the most expensive places in Rhadanthus, and the few that were genuinely good enough to eat in.

She counted the coins the mage had given her and almost dropped the letters. She held a small fortune in her hand, all navns, and one for every four letters!

With a quick look around, she dumped the coins back into the pouch and tucked it away inside her tunics, next to her skin.

She first delivered the letter to Lady Livian, this time just handing it to the servant at the door before running off. Then she set to work on the rest of the stack.

Delivering the rest of the letters took her the better part of the rest of the night, in part because several innkeepers were reluctant to let her enter, even when she displayed the letters as proof of her errand. She had to do a lot of convincing to complete her task.

When she finally stumbled into Shadow Keep candle-marks later, weary and footsore, she frowned at finding Aahmes leaning against a doorframe. He looked well-rested and cheerful. From his reaction as she approached, he must have been waiting for her.

"Late night, last night?" he inquired with a bright grin.

"Now, where would you get that idea?" Namid snarled at him.

He shrugged, still smiling. "I hope your wound isn't

paining you too much."

"I hope yours *is*," Namid said.

Aahmes just grinned more. "Don't forget you have just this day and night left. Time's running short."

"I'm not likely to forget how much time is left," she snapped. "Here." She tossed him two of the navns that Chendrukhar had given her. "Now shut up and leave me alone."

She pushed past him and headed for her room. Aahmes' laughter followed her.

CHAPTER 11

A loud thump jolted Namid from chaotic dreams. She propped herself up in her bed and looked around her room, not focusing well on anything. Hadn't she just fallen asleep?

She squinted at her door through sleep-fogged eyes, and spotted Thes' face. Dar's Second peered at her around the edge of her doorway.

"Are you awake?" he said.

"I am now. Sort of. How late is it?"

"About second candle-mark o' the afternoon."

"Second!" Namid started up, now wide awake. "How could I sleep so long?"

"Might be you were tired."

"Funny. What was that thump?" She said as she reluctantly pulled herself from her bed.

"Nothin' much. Dar's just got us changin' 'round a bit here and there. Guess there's new apprentices a-comin'."

"Oh. Couldn't you have done it a bit quieter?"

Thes shrugged, gave her a cheerful grin, and disappeared from her doorway. She sat a breath-of-time on her bed to collect her thoughts, then grabbed her cloak.

She hurried down to the kitchen, snatched something to eat, and left the Keep while still devouring her food.

Namid wandered through the streets, paying little attention to where her steps took her, as she tried to tally the things she would need for that night. She should have no trouble getting into the mage's hold. According to the letters she had delivered—Chendrukhar had not bothered to seal them so naturally she had read them—the celebration was to take place a day earlier, to accommodate the Lady Livian.

Namid smiled. It should be simplicity itself to get in during the bustle of arrivals and noisy entertainment that night.

When Namid bothered to notice where her steps had taken her, she found herself in front of a roper's shop. She realized that, although she had not planned it, she could not consider it an accident that she was there. A rope could be a handy thing to have, just in case. While she hoped it would not be necessary, she decided carrying a length of rope would be a good idea.

In the shop, she examined several before she decided on a length of a thin rope that the roper assured her was deceptively strong for its appearance. She silently thanked Chendrukhar for the navns when she heard the cost of the rope. She managed to haggle the price lower, but she still left with an emptier pouch.

She did not think she needed to buy anything else. She already had her tools for picking locks, clothing to help blend in with the night, and silent boots. A plan of Chendrukhar's hold would have been nice, but she knew she could never get one.

The next couple of candle-marks she spent in a deserted part of Rhadanthus testing her rope. The last thing she needed was for it to break that night.

The rope, however, was well-woven and held up to all she could think to do with it. She discovered that it had a slight give to it when she put some weight on it, but otherwise it performed just as she had expected.

When she finished her tests, she sought out Kaelior and borrowed her spyglass. Namid spent the rest of the time until dusk crouched on the town wall, examining the mage's wall and towers. The spyglass revealed nothing she had not already seen.

Watching the activity in the mage's courtyard, Namid experienced a pang of uncertainty. Chendrukhar was nothing like she had expected. Could she really steal the statue, something he probably valued? Misgivings at the thought bothered her.

A breath-of-time later, she chided herself for her foolishness. The statue would be missing just a few candle-marks, after all. He might not even notice its absence. And she was not about to let an intriguing face and an offer she had no intention of accepting get in the way of her chances at becoming a full Shadower.

After she returned the spyglass, Namid strolled back to the Keep, idly watching Rhadanthus assume its nighttime visage.

Along the way, a couple of men shouted lewd offers her direction, laughing the while. She ignored them. One of them persisted, until he found one of her stilettos at his throat. When she released him, he hurried away, melting back into the dusk shadows.

She encountered no further difficulties on her way back to the Keep.

Aahmes waited for her at the door.

"Got the Star yet?" he said with a wolfish grin.

She made a show of checking her pouches and looking around herself. "Seems not," she said and smiled back at him. "Patience, oh anxious Trial overseer. I still have time."

"Time that is growing shorter and shorter."

"Oh? You've noticed that too, huh?"

He glared at her. She hoped that meant she had at least somewhat irritated him by turning his taunts back on him.

"You won't be so cheerful at dawn."

"I won't?" She gave him her most innocent look. "Perhaps."

She brushed past him.

"We shall see, won't we?" she tossed back over her shoulder as she walked away.

She ate a quick meal in the solitude of her room, to avoid answering questions, well-meaning though they might be. She needed to be alone to focus on what she was about to do.

She anticipated that she might have to employ her own Power but hoped she could keep its use subtle and hidden. The ease with which Chendrukhar had called the two light orbs and controlled them gave her an idea of just how much Power he had at his command, and how well-practiced he was in its use.

She knew she did not want to oppose him directly.

After she finished eating, Namid changed into gray tunics and matching trousers, and braided her hair to keep it out of her way. Although short enough that a lot of stray strands stuck out of the braid, her hair was mostly contained at least.

She coiled her rope around her waist to keep it handy. She debated leaving her cloak behind, knowing that sometimes a cloak could get in the way. But as she thought of the cold of the previous night, she decided to wear it anyway. At least it was also a gray that would help her blend into the night.

After she checked to be sure she had everything she thought she might need, she slipped out of the Keep.

She paused in a dark alley to gather some Power and fashion a sense of non-presence around herself, in effect a kind of invisibility although people would still see her. They just would not think her presence unusual. It would be as if she belonged there, like a servant.

She doubted it would be of any help if she came face to face with Chendrukhar, but she hoped it would turn aside casual glances from his people and his guests. A passive use of Power, and set up a good distance from the mage, he should not be able to sense her through her use of it.

That done, she hurried through the city to the East Gate, taking back streets and alleys to reach her destination. She waited near the gate, but out of sight, until a group of nobles approached – probably headed to the mage's gathering. When the gatekeeper's attention turned to them, she slipped out of Rhadanthus.

CHAPTER 12

The mage's hold was brightly lit for the festivities, unlike the night before. Namid approached at a slow walk to give herself plenty of time to study the situation. One tower looked unlit. The taller one. She decided that would be the place to look for the statue.

Getting into the hold was as simple as she had hoped. She followed a small group of guests, and when they passed a recessed area in the courtyard, she slipped into the meager shadows there. For several long breaths-of-time, she remained still and watched the activity, trying to pick out any patterns of motion.

She spotted Chendrukhar once, but lost sight of him again in the frenzy of arriving guests and hurrying servants. After she had waited as long as she dared, she left her alcove and made her way around the perimeter of the bustle, trying to act like she belonged there.

She found the door set into the wall that ran from the shorter of the lighted towers to the outer wall of the hold. She checked the door—unlocked—and used it to escape the lights.

On the other side, Namid found herself in darkness,

but as her eyes adjusted, she realized that she stood in yet another courtyard. And there stood the unlit tower, no more than ten paces in front of her. She approached it in silence, all senses alert for any guardians, human or otherwise. She reached the tower without incident and circled it. When she reached the point where she had started her circle, she made a quiet sound of dismay. She had found no door! She looked up and saw that one bridge connected this tower to one of the others.

Hadn't she seen more than a single connecting bridge earlier?

She frowned and repeated her circuit of the tower. This time she trailed one hand along the smooth stones, with her other senses open to detect any traces of Power that might conceal a door. And she discovered nothing different.

Namid cursed in a quiet voice, then returned to the outer courtyard and slipped into the door in the short tower that she had spotted on her first visit. She followed a servant back and forth until she had located the rooms in use for the party. Then she retraced her steps to a shadowy, curved staircase she had noticed earlier, and started up.

When she reached the first landing, Namid paused to catch her breath. She had climbed more than three hundred steps! But from the outside, the tower had not looked that tall. Power must be involved. She suspected to discourage exactly what she was attempting.

She flung a defiant thought into the darkness and eased open the single door on the landing.

Namid closed the door behind her, taking care to make no noise, and looked down the hall in which she found herself. Torches in unevenly spaced sconces on the walls lit the undecorated hall of light gray stone... floors, walls, and ceiling.

Namid thought this might be the bridge to the tower she wanted but knew of no way to verify this other than to go see. So, she headed down the hall, cautious and alert.

Without warning, and sooner than she had expected, she reached the end of the hall. From where she had started, it had seemed to stretch much further.

She grabbed the closest torch and peered through the archway she faced.

Like trying to look through black velvet, she thought.

She thrust the torch in front of her, to no avail. She could not penetrate the blackness. Namid gazed back down the long-looking hallway and considered her options. Then she replaced the torch, faced the darkness, and closed her eyes. She gathered Power to herself, a little at a time, just a trickle taken from the Power she could feel in the night. She hoped gathering Power so slowly would keep Chendrukhar from noticing her use of it.

When her skin started to tingle with the accumulation of Power, she opened her eyes and tried to impress the Power with her desire to see clearly, to see through any illusion that might exist to the reality beneath. For a long breath-of-time, Namid met resistance and the darkness prevailed. Then with a faint sound like tearing cloth, the darkness split in the middle and cascaded to either side.

With a gasp, Namid jumped back from the lip of the precipice that she now saw at her feet. After she managed to calm her sudden fear, she edged forward to peer out and down. From the look of it, she stood at the top of a tower. One step further would have dropped her to her death in the courtyard.

Trembling from how close she had come to disaster, she still took the opportunity to look around, to see what she might discover to help her. From her vantage, she could just see part of the darkened tower to her left and back the direction she had come. She also spotted part of a bridge, closer to the ground and definitely connected at one end to the darkened tower.

That must be the bridge she truly wanted. But how to get to it?

Still trembling, she retraced her steps up the hall.

As she neared the door through which she had entered the hall, she spotted another next to it, set in the wall of the hallway-bridge. Illusion must have previously concealed this second door and her recent use of Power now let her see through it. Unlike the other door, this one was locked.

She pulled her lockpicks from their hidden pocket within her belt and set to work. A few breaths-of-time later, she tucked them away again, then gave the door a gentle push.

The door swung away from her, revealing another hall, similar to the one in which she stood but with far fewer torches lighting it. At the far end stood a closed door. The walls and floor of the new hallway wavered several times, then solidified. Namid wondered what illusion she was looking through.

One hand still on the door handle, she eased into the hall, looking around for any surprises... and stifled a cry as the floor vanished from under her feet. She grabbed frantically for the door handle with her free hand and managed to catch it before her other hand slipped off. Cursing under her breath, she pulled herself back up into the first hallway.

When she looked back, that false hallway still looked as solid as before.

Namid backed away from the doorway, her heart pounding in her ears from the sudden jolt of fear the fall had given her. Her heel caught on something and she pitched backward... right through the wall behind her.

With a barely stifled curse, she landed hard on a stone floor and scrambled right back to her feet. A quick spin around showed her that she stood in yet another hallway. She could see a foggy version of the wall she had fallen through. It resembled a thin curtain with markings like stone on it. Her hand passed through it easily when she tried to touch it. She stepped back into the first hall and closed the door to the deceptive hall.

She then studied the illusion—or she assumed that it was illusion—that hid the new hall. The spot she had fallen through looked no different from the rest of the wall. A stronger illusion that her Power couldn't penetrate? With a shrug, she walked back through that section of the wall then paused to study this latest hallway.

Gray stone like the others, this hall contained a few widely spaced torches. Windows made up one wall. When Namid looked out, she saw the courtyard below her. It looked much closer than it had seemed earlier. The door at the end of the hall stood just a few paces away. She hoped it would lead into the dark tower.

But walking toward it brought her no closer to her goal. And whatever the Power was doing now, it did not involve illusion. Namid stopped several long breaths-of-time to think, then looked back the way she had come.

The opening through which she had fallen was within an armlength of her. Something prompted her to step toward it, and it seemed to move further away from her. Another step and it retreated further.

She glanced over her shoulder at the door she wanted to reach. It was now the same distance closer to her that the opening had seemed to move away from her.

Namid continued this strange journey until a glance back showed the door within reach behind her. Only then did she wonder if continuing in this manner would allow her to pass through the door, or if she would be trapped in this hall forever.

She suppressed the shiver of fear that thought gave her. She took one last step and almost fell as she bumped into the door behind her. It opened of its own accord and she stood in a small room, looking through the door and down the hall she had just traversed.

The door swung shut, faded away and left her facing the appearance of a blank wall. Namid suppressed another shudder and looked around the room. The light from a single torch showed her an empty room with neither windows nor doors. And no illusion that she could sense.

Namid examined all the walls, taking her time. When she still had not discovered a way out, she sat on the floor and studied the walls from that angle and distance. When she *still* saw no way out, she slumped, dropping her head to her hands. She tried to fight down a wave of despair as she saw her chances of becoming a full Shadower dissolve into dust.

And she could not think of a way even the Power could help.

What could she possibly be missing?

CHAPTER 13

Namid sat on the cold, stone floor, curled in on herself and floundering in self-pity. But after many long breaths-of-time of this, she cursed herself for a fool and turned her gaze upward. There, no more than three or so paces above her, tucked up nice and neat against the ceiling, was a ladder.

Namid jumped to her feet and walked the ladder's length while examining it. As far as she could tell, she should be able to pull on one end to rotate it down so that it reached from the floor to the ceiling. And near its other end, she spotted a telltale square in the ceiling that marked the way out.

If she could just reach the one end to pull it down.

After some thought about how best to do that, Namid uncoiled her new rope and tied one end to one of her daggers, the one with the longest blade. She grasped the rope not far from that end and whirled it around.

Pain shot through her arm as she released the rope and only the side of the dagger struck the bottom rung of the ladder. The dagger fell to the floor with a loud clang. Namid jumped at the sudden noise. She cursed Aahmes and the wound he had given her while she looked around. No sign that anyone had heard. Yet.

She plucked the dagger from the floor and balanced it in her other hand. One of her other knives would have been better for throwing, but if anyone had heard the noise, she had only breaths-of-time to get out.

After a pause to better judge the distance, she threw the dagger upward, with the smallest push of Power to guide it and give it force. It lodged in a lower rung and she wasted no time in pulling on the rope to lower that end down. The ladder's other end remained attached to the ceiling next to the trap door.

Namid retrieved her dagger from where it lodged in the ladder, gathered the rope, and dashed up the ladder. With some difficulty, she opened the door, then pulled herself up into yet another room. As she closed the door, she saw the ladder begin to swing back to the ceiling beneath her.

This new room was dark, but as Namid stood there, a slight glow emanated from the ceiling and revealed a door to her left. She rewrapped her rope around her waist but continued to hold her dagger. She reached out to the door, which opened at her touch. She peered through.

The door led to another room, this one candlelit. A long, narrow table stood at the far side, next to the wall. Namid smiled at the sight of the silvery object atop the table next to the candle: the Star of Corentris. She was surprised to see that the statue stood just a couple of hands tall. She had pictured it taller.

Before she stepped through the door, Namid studied the shadowed room, looking for any signs of traps. She discovered nothing, so she approached the table and reached for the statue, with every intention of grabbing it and running.

The statue moved.

Namid froze, stifling a shriek of surprise.

Did she really see that?

She took another step toward it. Yes, it moved.

The statue elongated and stretched upward, growing larger as it did. It looked less like a distorted star and took on a sort of person-like shape. The top half of the statue leaned toward her. It looked like it was bowing to her.

She suppressed a nervous giggle at the thought.

She sheathed the dagger she still carried. Without thinking, without knowing why, she put out her hand. A tiny dagger, just about the length of her longest finger, dropped into her palm. Between one breath-of-time and the next, the dagger became full-sized. The statue resumed its normal shape and size.

Namid stared at the Star. When it did nothing else, she sidled over to it and reached out, ready to flee if it moved again. But it kept still, and kept its normal size and normal, somewhat star-shaped form.

When she touched the Star, Namid had the unnerving sensation that something else now occupied the room with her. Gripping the statue in her left hand, she turned.

The apparition she faced was unlike anything she had ever seen. She would have thought it came straight from some nether realm if she had believed in such a place. The creature—for she felt it *was* alive—had no true shape, but was rather a hulking darkness, a black vapor that seethed in front of her. Namid saw nothing that looked like eyes, but she knew that its attention was fixed on her.

It roiled toward her without a sound, carrying with it a reek of rottenness. One part of it flowed faster and reached out for her.

Without thinking, she swiped at it, only somewhat aware that she used the hand that held the dagger from the statue. She winced as a sharp pang from the slice Aahmes had given her shot through her arm at her motion.

The creature rolled and boiled away from her to avoid the touch of the dagger. Another tendril snapped out at her and brushed her left shoulder before she could bring the dagger around.

She gasped at the sudden agony from that touch. A

creeping numbness followed the pain and spread from the point the creature had touched.

The sudden clang of the Star hitting the floor shattered the eerie silence of the conflict. Namid froze, watching the creature.

Why had it stopped? Why was it failing to continue the attack?

The creature shifted back and forth, acting like it was trying to break free of some restraint, and Namid suspected that the mage had tasked it with holding her there—well, any intruder, she suspected—until he could arrive.

She kept her gaze on the creature as she retrieved the Star and shoved the statue one-handed into a sack at her waist. She secured the top of the sack the best she could, with one hand almost completely numb. Then she darted for the door.

When she moved, the nightmare flowed right behind her. It flicked a tendril at her but missed. Just barely.

Outside the door, instead of the room she had entered through, Namid faced a hallway. In the faint glow from the ceiling, she saw no trapdoor in the floor, nor any doors along the walls. The hall looked long, much longer than should have been possible in the tower.

Namid glanced over her shoulder and ducked as the creature reached for her again. The tendril lightly brushed her leg as she scrambled to get away. She barely held back a scream at the agony that stabbed through her at the touch. Again, a creeping numbness spread from the spot, but much slower this time.

She stumbled down the hall, trying to move as fast as she could, hoping to find a way out—at the end, if not sooner—before the creature caught her. As she fled, she felt the new dagger shrinking in her hand until it was again just finger-length. She dropped it into the sack with the Star to keep from losing it.

And she fled.

After long breaths-of-time that seemed more like candle-marks, she saw a door at the far end of the hall. She did not dare look behind to see how close the creature was for fear of losing ground. She tried to move even faster and, at last, crashed into the door that she had seen. She tried the handle and grinned when it opened without effort. And she stopped herself right before she stepped off into the air and took a long drop to the courtyard below.

She teetered there on the brink of a terrifying fall, then she caught her balance and her breath. Her heart pounded, and her hands shook in reaction. She looked over her shoulder, back down the hall.

The creature still followed but was further back than she had expected. But between it and the drop to the courtyard, she was trapped. She looked around in search of inspiration.

How to get out of this?

An oddity at her feet caught her attention. Was that a slight blurriness between her and the courtyard, just beyond where her toes hung over the edge of the doorsill? To either side of the doorway the courtyard looked clear and crisp.

She reached out with one foot without putting her weight on it and felt a solid floor there. Although she could not see it.

Keeping hold of the door handle—just in case—Namid eased forward less than half a pace and ran into something about knee-high in front of her. She released the door handle and explored the unseen obstacle with both hands—although her left hand and arm were still mostly numb. She decided the obstacle felt like a metal latticework railing. She reached over and felt no floor beyond it. A quick glance back down the hallway and she saw that the creature still followed her, closing the distance.

She closed the door, uncoiled her rope and tied one

end to the unseen railing. Working as fast as she could, she fashioned herself a crude harness with a waist belt and leg loops from the other end of the rope. She hoped that she did it right, the way Dar had shown her. By feel, she clambered over the unseen railing, dropped the rest of the rope down, hoping that it would be long enough, and started the long climb down.

Namid had gone no more than a couple of paces when the door above slammed open and the creature boiled out toward her. Keeping her gaze on the thing, she sped up, going as fast as she dared. Her wounded arm burned from the strain and she thought she felt blood beneath that armguard.

She slipped many times, having trouble gripping the rope with her half-numb hand. She cursed under her breath all the while but stayed ahead of the thing. At least it seemed to need the rope just as she did, clinging to it to descend toward to the ground much as she was.

A celebratory urge washed over her when her feet finally touched the ground. Rather than try to untie herself, she sliced through the rope with a handy dagger and stumbled toward the door that led back to the main courtyard. Both hands stung from burns from slipping on the rope, but she ignored the added pain in her need to escape.

Just breaths-of-time ahead of the creature, Namid reached the door and yanked it open, heedless of who might be beyond. She stumbled through the doorway and slipped into the shadows that ringed the courtyard. She let out the breath she had not realized she was holding when the few people left in the courtyard took no notice of her. The sense of non-presence she had placed around herself still held.

A glance back showed her the creature halted in the doorway she had just come through. Maybe it could not leave that part of the mage's hold.

She hoped that was true.

She hurried around the edge of the lighted courtyard and out the gate. And she ran, still stumbling frequently, all the way back to the city, wanting to put as much distance as she could, as fast as she could, between her and the mage and his creature.

The guard at the gate to Rhadanthus owed her a favor and so made no fuss about letting her in so late, although he did study her with a worried expression. She almost smiled as she imagined the picture she must present. She hurried away from him before he could question her and headed through the streets toward Shadow Keep.

Some distance shy of the Keep, Namid found an alcove in which to take refuge. After she stopped shaking, after she made sure she was not leaving a trail of blood, she took some time to admire the statue, then tucked it back in the sack.

She pulled the tiny dagger from the sack and tucked it into her belt with her lockpicks until she could decide what she wanted to do with it.

She did not want to return to the Keep too soon. Closer to dawn would do, so she settled in to wait. No need to make it look too easy. Without meaning to, she dozed then while she waited for time to pass.

Roughly a candle-mark before dawn, Namid left her alcove and sauntered to the main entrance to Shadow Keep, pleased to find that the numbness from the creature's touch had dissipated. A figure detached itself from the shadows near the Keep door and approached her. She noticed rustlings and murmurs around her as other Shadowers edged closer.

Namid stepped up to the figure… Aahmes, of course. She was not at all surprised that he was there to meet her.

"Well?" he said.

Namid untied the sack from her belt and handed it to him. The others edged even closer as Aahmes loosened the top of the sack. Namid watched his face as he looked within. His eyes flicked to hers for just an instant and she thought she saw a hint of admiration in his expression.

Not likely....

She told herself she must have imagined it.

Aahmes reached into the sack and pulled out the statue. He held it high so all the Shadowers could see.

And Namid had trouble keeping to her feet as everyone jostled to congratulate her. The press of the crowd took her through the door into their home.

"Your turn!" Namid called to Aahmes over her shoulder, just before she lost sight of him.

~

NOTES AND PRONUNCIATIONS

A week is eight days long.

A "candle-mark" is roughly equivalent to an hour.

A "breath-of-time" is an indeterminate short amount of time, roughly seconds to a few minutes.

A "pace" is the length of a double step (roughly five feet).

Aahmes -- AH mehz
Aerill -- AY rihl

Biera -- BYAYR uh

Carssi -- KAHR see
Chendrukhar -- CHEHN droo kahr
Corentris -- kohr EHN trihss

Dar -- DAHR

Edmer -- EHD mer
Elnathan -- EL nuh thuhn

Falgien -- FAL gyehn

Jai -- JAY
Jaikrein -- JAY kr-eye-n

Kaelior -- KAY lee ohr
Keizha -- K-EYE zhuh
korz -- KOHRZ
Kundu -- KOON doo

Livian -- LIH vee uhn

TRIAL RUN

Macai -- MAH kay
Milda -- MIHL duh

Namid -- NAH meed
navn -- NAH vuhn

Orran -- OH ruhn

Paronia -- puh ROHN yuh

Rhadanthus -- ruh DAN thuhss

Saward -- SAH wahrd
Surbhi -- SUR bee

Thes -- THEHSS
Tige -- TIHJ
Tun-Lir -- tuhn LEER

Uffke -- OOV keh

Zwena -- ZWEHN uh

~

AUTHOR'S NOTE

Thank you for reading my book. I hope you enjoyed it!

Please consider leaving an honest review on the book's
product page at your favorite online bookstore
and on Goodreads. Reviews from readers like you are
powerful and greatly help other readers
discover books they might enjoy.

-Lynn

ABOUT THE AUTHOR

S. Lynn Helton lives in the foothills of the Rocky
Mountains, U.S.A., with her family and a couple of crazy
cats. Lynn enjoys camping and hiking, playing games,
crafting, reading (a lot) and, of course, writing.

Read more about her books on her website:
www.slynnhelton.com